As i

Sophie Parkin

BEST
OF
FRIENDS

True stories of
friendships that
blossomed or bombed

PICCADILLY PRESS • LONDON

To all my best friends.
Lots of love, Sophie.

First published in Great Britain in 2006
by Piccadilly Press Ltd.,
5 Castle Road, London NW1 8PR
www.piccadillypress.co.uk

ISBN: 1 85340 848 4 (trade paperback)
ISBN-13: 9 781853 408489

1 3 5 7 9 10 8 6 4 2

Printed and bound in Great Britain by Bookmarque Ltd
Cover design by Simon Davis and Sue Hellard
Typeset by M Rules, London

Set in Stone Serif and Melanie

Contents

INTRODUCTION

Talking to all the girls and women in this book has made me realise one thing: that best friends might not be for life, but each friendship is unique. Meeting and listening to each of the interviewees has been fascinating.

I was very fortunate to be invited into Jasmine Guinness's beautiful home only weeks after she gave birth, for tea with chocolate cake. Sophie Ellis-Bextor had just finished recording and was still lipstick-immaculate while being mummy to her son. Cathy Hopkins was madly busy writing books in her garden shed, trying to find her glasses amongst her cats. Funny and frank Trisha Goddard was in her office, rushing between the gym and a photoshoot before hopping off on holiday. I laughed with wise and sassy Irma Kurtz in the Maison Bertaux, Soho, with demure Daisy de Villeneuve, and with sweet Charlotte Cooper, just back for a week while touring in the States. Vanessa Fenton squeezed me in between a perform-ance of *Swan Lake* and a glass of champagne, measuring every word. I met my MP, the enigmatic

Kate Hoey, in the House of Commons over a cup of herbal tea, and I was sung to by the amazing Karen O. Each of their stories reveals more than any interview I've read with any of these women, because a best friend is a direct reflection of you, whatever age you are.

Whether you are looking back at your friendships from a distance with insight and detachment, like many of these women, or immersed in the quagmire of full-bloodied teenage emotions, like Beatrice, Katy, Florrie, Jenny, Giselle, Becky, Carmen, Amelia, Flic, Daisy, Katrina, Lana and Ruby, best friends are unforgettable, even if they haven't lasted – and many in these stories haven't.

A best friend should be kind, funny, forgiving, great at keeping secrets and sharing theirs. They will accept your foibles and enjoy your successes as if they were their own. They will be proud of you and tolerant, understanding and generous. In fact, they will be all the things that you are to them!

With a best friend you can laugh so much you think you might wet yourself, and that just makes you laugh even more. You can cry on their shoulder about a boy until their jacket needs the tumble-drier, and they won't complain – they'll understand, even if it's over their brother.

Best friends often make up secret languages together, better to keep the world out. They finish each other's sentences, wear the same clothes, share the same beliefs, fancy the same boys and giggle at the same jokes. They share their highest hopes, even dreams, and their darkest fears and secrets.

For a lucky few, best friends last their whole lives. For others, a best friend sees them through times when their own families disappoint (they're not cool enough, funny enough, clever enough; they're just not enough!). Suddenly, a best friend is worth more than any amount of money.

When you stop seeing your best friend's point of view, or vice versa, you know things might be falling apart, but even if the friendship ends really badly, that can't take away all the really good things that a best friend once gave you when you needed it most.

I must say a special thank you to everyone who gave me the time, energy, honesty and trust to share their unique story with me, even when they didn't want their real name used – you know who you are. Also, to all the female role models who give us the inspiration to achieve even a small amount of what they have done in their lives, from making music or books, to fighting our causes.

Sophie Parkin

SUMMER WITH MAY

FLORRIE, 15

I liked May the first time we met, at a party. She was giggly and she had weird, sticky-out hair, a darker version of my blond hair. We had friends that knew each other who introduced us, and we got on straight away. I guess it was because we were both a bit freaky, and didn't dress like everyone else. She was straightforward, but she didn't mind being different in the way she looked.

We don't go to the same school. May goes to the posh private school down the hill from mine. Not everyone who goes there is posh, but you do have to pay, and her family have more money than mine. I go to the big comprehensive, but all the kids in our year from all the schools in the area meet up – either around the station after school in the winter, because there's a mall to keep warm in; or in the park during the summer. When it's warm we love to just hang in the park, talking and lying on the grass. The boys play football and us girls pretend we're watching. As if! We have far too many important things to discuss other than the state of the boys' legs and bums, though that can be interesting too.

It was still spring when I met May. At first, we saw each other a few times with other friends like Jack and Enya and we'd just cotch together, you know, hang out. We all liked art, we'd go to galleries after school, like the National Portrait Gallery or the Tate Modern. At that time there was this giant orange sun mirrored in the ceiling of the Turbine Hall, called the Weather Project and we would go and lie on the floor staring at our reflections, talking for hours. We always had so much fun when we were together.

The only problems were, May lived miles away, and she had a really weird dad. May told me that he was always drunk, and he definitely looked like he was whenever I saw him. He always had a drink in his hand. Plus, getting to the station near May's was a nightmare, and then it still took ages to walk to her house. She wasn't one of those convenient friends who live just around the corner.

So May started staying around my house at week-ends. Her dad didn't mind at first, then he started taking it personally, thinking I was taking May away from him; it was weird. So that left meeting after school or going to hers, but her dad was so freaky it was really awkward.

We'd have long phone chats or go on MSN Messenger to stay in touch. We liked the same things –

neither of us can play a musical instrument but we love music. Music and laughing! We were always watching comedies together, and eating strawberry cheesecake ice cream. Sometimes we'd go to TopShop for the whole day. Neither of us had any money but we'd spend the whole day trying on clothes for fun, until the assistants would tell us to get lost. When we were hungry we'd go into the deli stall in the supermarket and pretend we wanted to test bits of pies and cheese and anchovies. We spent hours putting on make-up, experimenting on each other or ourselves – like the time we painted our nails with Tippex and drew felt-tip pictures over them. Have you ever tried getting Tippex off your nails? I don't recommend it. We liked cooking, and when we baked some bread for her school science experiment we were determined to eat it, too. I'm not sure what we forgot to do, but trying to eat the stuff almost cracked our teeth.

It was soon the summer holidays. May was the first friend I'd ever had that I didn't mind spending long periods of time with – because we had so much fun. Other friends always irritate me after a whole day together – they'll say something stupid, or they don't think before they speak and you have to deal with so much rubbish anyway, I don't need it from friends too. I tell them, "Sorry, you're making me really mad. I can't stay around you, I need a rest." I'll tell them to go home, if they're getting on my nerves, or I'll go home. But it was never like that with May. We had a whole summer of fun and no school and just hanging about in the park talking and laughing, laughing and talking, whistling through grass, or making daisy chains. That was, until we met Ruben.

Ruben was sixteen and we were thirteen when we all first met. He doesn't go to either of our schools, and he used to do drugs but he's cleaned himself up and he's doing his A-levels now. I thought he was great when I first met him – he seemed a lot of fun and he had this great big wild afro. Sometimes we'd go round to his house and listen to music – he's wicked at playing the guitar, and he'd graffitied a fantastic mural all over his bedroom wall. He was really changing his life because he knew he'd been wasting his time on drugs and wanted to do good. I like people when they realise they can change things for themselves. I guess May did too.

Ruben lives closer to May than me. She began dropping over to his house alone after school, then at weekends. Whenever I called her up and asked where she was, it was always – "Oh, I'm just round at Ruben's."

May said he wasn't her boyfriend, but I couldn't believe it. She said she spent time around there because he was teaching her how to tag (design her graffiti name). Whatever. We both turned fourteen that summer but by September there seemed to be more and more times when she was busy around Ruben's and couldn't see me.

What can you do? I've got lots of other friends so it's not like I'm going to be alone; I just spent more time with Tania and Poppy.

One day May told me that she'd had sex with Ruben, and I knew that was the end. Things had changed, she had changed. She'd become less like May and more like one of Ruben's belongings. They won't even come out with us now because Ruben says, now he's seventeen, he doesn't want his friends to see him hanging with fourteen-year-olds. He doesn't even take her out.

May speaks to him every night on the phone for two hours, and that's after dropping by his place for an hour after school. He's not that interesting, but May's kind of obsessive like that.

The summer seems a long time ago. Now it's so cold. I can't believe our garden is coated in snow. The snow has a way of separating you from remembering the sun. I know there are going to be other summers, I'll have another great time with my friends this coming summer, but it's not going to be the same without May. If you don't know, I can't explain what it's like to have a friend who wants and likes all the things you do; who says what you're thinking, or does something before you say it; a friend you want to be with because she makes everything better than it was before; who's not afraid of looking silly and doesn't get embarrassed.

I'll never forget May on the hottest day ever. You could see the haze making everything shimmer. It was so hot I had to lie in the shade under a tree, too exhausted to move. May, dressed in a cut-off jean skirt and T-shirt, leaped up and started doing cartwheels about the lawn before she leaped into the mini fountain and did a handstand. Everybody could see her polka-dot knickers. She began the largest water fight ever seen – we all joined in. The park keeper chased everyone out for causing a disturbance. All of us were soaked, and none of us could stop laughing. For ages we were curled up on the pavement, cracking up.

Then there was the time a gang of rude girls tried to jack us for our phones and she shouted at them so loudly they ran away.

You can keep on remembering these times, but what's the point?

I don't know, I really liked May, and we kept talking for a while, but it's not the same. I know she's been saying things about me behind my back to Poppy, like I'm jealous of her and Ruben, that I fancy him and just rubbish stuff, but she won't say them to me and I really don't like that. Why can't she be straight? She's changed and as long as Ruben's around, she's going to spend all her time with him.

The other day I bumped into her and we had

nothing to say to each other, except: "Are you going to see the gig on Saturday night?" "No. It's sold out." That was it! I could never have imagined we would lose our connection; that our friendship would be empty and meaningless. We hadn't even disagreed, there isn't even an argument to fight over. I can't feel angry. It's like I've lost something – I'm not even sure what it was – but it's gone now. At least we don't go to the same school or live near each other, so we don't have to see each other every day.

Maybe it was one of those special summer things you always remember – 'That Summer With May'. Maybe when I'm a hundred and five, I'll wonder, "Whatever happened to May?" Or maybe we'll bump into each other again when we're both grown up. One day we'll both be working in Paris or living in New York, maybe even Mexico, and I'll be walking down some street, or sitting in a restaurant, or café and suddenly we'll recognise something about each other at exactly the same time. We'll scream, "HELLO!", hug each other and then we'll become instant best friends all over again, without saying a thing about what happened all those years before. I'd like that, really like that. That would be so good, to become best friends with May all over again. That would be cool.

THE COOL GANG

TRISHA GODDARD, TV PRESENTER,
TALK SHOW HOST AND PRODUCER
Trishatv.com

I had never fitted in. I never felt that I fitted in at school, or with my family. My skin was always darker than my siblings and years later I discovered why: because my dad was not my biological dad.

My teenage years were a time of such great change. It was 1969, the Swinging Sixties, when I got into my posh all-girl selective grammar school in Chertsey, Surrey. I won a place there because I was bright, but of course that made me a swot, and I so didn't want to be a swot. I wanted to be part of the cool, trendy crowd.

All the trendy, cool girls were rich, they could afford all the latest fashions. My parents were poor, we had no money and while that didn't matter when I was at home, it did matter when I was with my friends from school. Luckily, Mum was a great seamstress and she would copy all the latest fashions. My clothes might not have had the labels but, boy, I had the look.

Both my mum and dad were psychiatric nurses, lowest of the low jobs at that time, but my dad didn't just do that. To make enough money to look after us all he worked two jobs, sometimes gardening for some of my friends' rich families. I used to beg him not to work for people I knew. I was hideously ashamed of my family at school. I wanted so much to belong.

There were a few of us 'poor ones' at our school who either lived in council housing or accommodation that came with our parents' jobs, as our house did. Instead of coming together as a group, we were all fiercely competitive, not just academically but socially too. We all wanted to be best friends with Evelyn and Katrin, the cool girls. I suppose Sue (a girl whose parents at least owned their modest bungalow!) and I were the closest to the cool gang and in an odd way we were also the closest to each other as friends. I always thought at that time that I didn't have a 'best friend' but now I realise I did. It was Sue. We lived fairly close to each other, but it wasn't just a friendship of convenience.

Sue was the friend I did all my teenage experimenting with, getting drunk, smoking and getting off with boys, when we were both fifteen. We'd each egg the other on to be naughtier and more badly behaved. It was all part of our undeclared competitive friendship. Spurred on by neither of us wanting to be dworks, we were trapped together in this hinterland of trying. We both reminded each other where we weren't quite cool enough; we were almost perfect reflections of the other.

I kept diaries all the way through those years. I documented my anxieties and what I now see as obvious depression and being on the verge of an eating disorder. I just stopped eating. I had been a tubby, happy girl growing up, but I knew if I wanted to be cool and wear the latest fashions, I had to be thin. The only thing I ate was breakfast, and that was a swig of sherry off the top of the cabinet and a Digestive biscuit. At lunch and dinner I'd just push the food around my plate, never really eating any of it. Nobody knew or talked of eating disorders in those days, but because my parents both worked in a psychiatric hospital they knew more about them than most. In fact, there was a girl at my school who was admitted with anorexia, seriously underweight. At one point I lost so much weight, and neither Mum or Dad could make me eat, that my father said if I was going to behave like a baby he was going to treat me like one. Unless I ate, he would drive me everywhere to conserve my energy. He thought I started eating because I didn't want to appear babyish in front of all my friends, but the truth was that I was so ashamed of our reconditioned second-hand army cadet car I couldn't bear the thought of my friends seeing me driving around in it. I was such a snob! Honestly, if he'd had a Bentley I would have loved to be chauffeured about.

I came from a working-class family. Sue came from a middle-class family. Her dad was an architect and her mum was a teacher. I had to have a Saturday job from the age of fifteen. I was expected to bring money into the home as soon as I was old enough to work, because there were six of us in our tiny house. Sue just had one sister, and her mum washed and ironed and did everything for her, even when she was sixteen. It seemed to me that her parents were forever hugging and kissing and asking her opinion on things, communicating as parents should, but that world was so foreign to me. I used to sit and marvel at the way they behaved and interacted together. Our home seemed more like a kind of boarding house where things revolved around my exhausted parents' night-duty schedules and arguing. It felt like we were all expected to just get on with it. As for open displays of affection – I never recall my parents holding hands, let alone kissing or hugging each other.

My parents' childhoods had been tough. Mum's father had died when she was three and while her mother worked full-time, she was placed in a boarding school. My dad had a rural Norfolk childhood – he left school at fourteen and had to go and earn a living. I might have been envious of the family lives of friends like Katrin, Evelyn and Sue but I knew I was better equipped to survive and earn money in the outside world. The others seemed so mollycoddled to me.

Still, being with Sue allowed me a greater amount

of freedom than I was ever allowed at home. After we finished our exams, Evelyn, the really cool one, and me were invited by Sue to go and stay in Brighton for a holiday with her cousin who was an air stewardess and her teacher boyfriend. In those days being an air stewardess was the epitome of glamour and we were very excited. Sue's parents drove us down and we were read the riot act by her mum when we arrived:

No answering back or being cheeky.

Wash up after meals.

Regular baths.

Early bedtime.

We thought, "God, this is going to be an awful holiday." Then, as soon as Sue's mum left, the boyfriend appeared and said, "So who minds if I skin up a joint?" Suddenly we realised we were going to have fun. We spent a week getting drunk and getting off with boys. We were completely feral – we didn't even bother with showering. I remember one evening waking up because the phone wouldn't stop ringing and nobody else was answering so I picked up the phone and it was my dad. "Trisha, is that you?" he said, and I was lying there with a boy. I had to put my hand over the boy's mouth to stop him talking, in case my father heard.

One night we even rang up our friends in the pub near where we lived back home and told them all to come down for a party. The entire bar of The Green

Man pub arrived and we partied all night. It was the most debauched holiday I have ever had.

I think of that as our last summer together. After that, things changed between Sue and me. I left school to go and work in a TV costumiers in London. We were in a band together, called Eve. I played keyboards – I'd been playing piano since I was five – and Sue played drums. I remember thinking that she was getting to be difficult, argumentative and unfocused, and that I was ready to leave Sue behind. That even though she was amazingly creative and a fantastic artist and a great drummer, she was holding us back. When our manager decided she'd have to go, I quite clinically agreed. I'd learned communication skills from working in the outside world and she seemed babyish and hard work. I got sick of the rows. The band was renamed The Mothertrucker; we were gigging a lot, but Sue was too much. We had a meeting and she was sacked. Her mother heard and came in shouting at all of us, how Sue had dropped out of Sixth Form to tour Germany, that we couldn't drop her. I'll never forget her turning round to point at me, saying, "And you're a traitor! You're meant to be her best friend."

Horribly guilty though I felt, I still thought I was right. It was the right decision. She was a troubled soul.

The thing is, I've brought my own children up not

as I was by my parents but, I suppose, more in the vein of Sue's family: we're very huggy-touchy and I believe in treating my kids as children.

I did see Sue again. My show organised a surprise reunion of the band – Maureen, Annie and Sue. I was shocked to say the least. It was nice to know what everyone else was doing, but I'm very happy to leave it there, in the '70s, part of being a teenager. I corresponded for a while with Sue but I don't think I could be close to her now – sometimes you have to leave people behind. I can be quite hard-headed and tough about protecting myself. That was then and this, this is now.

A Missing Part

Jenny, 19

When we met, I thought we were the same person. Honestly, for a moment it was like looking in a mirror. Obviously not when I took a proper look, but for that first second. We were the same in so many ways it was as if I already knew her. I thought that when we met we would be together forever, almost as if Josie was a missing part of me that I'd lost when I was a kid.

You know, I can't even remember now what it was like before I met Josie. I know she changed my life when I had thought it couldn't be changed anymore because it had already been changed so much, and for the worse; more than I could bear.

When I was fifteen, my parents had this great idea to get in touch with their inner fieldmice and move from the city into the middle of nowhere in the countryside. Great!

How do parents come up with these brilliant and innovative ideas? Why did they think it would be so good for all of us? When I was just old enough to start getting into clubs without an ID, I was moved to a place without a club for miles. I had reached the age of fun, friends and freedom, just to have my face smacked down into a cowpat – *and* I had to leave my new boyfriend, Tommy, behind, not to mention all my friends. Friends I'd known since I was four. Plus, my brother wasn't even coming;, he was staying put and leaving home. Or rather he was staying and we were leaving. What were they thinking? I knew Dad had got a new job, but couldn't he have found one in the city? But no, it had to be in the country.

So, suddenly my life was replaced with huge green fields threaded with tiny country roads and patch-worked with black and white cows. The fields were surrounded by sea, sand and sky, which is nice theo-retically, BUT I had no friends. Not one. The sky was constantly full of billowing clouds that in seconds would grow grey, probably provoked by sheer bore-dom – they had to be as miserable as me.

I know. Why couldn't I have gone out and made some new friends? I could have if we weren't five miles from the nearest shop, eight miles from a tiny town. There just weren't other people nearby and the only transport I had was a bicycle. At times it seemed like being in prison would be better. I'm not joking. We didn't even have any electricity – we had candles. We had gone from a normal, modern existence to a stone-age lifestyle. Laugh if you like, but it wasn't funny.

In September I started at the local college to do my A-levels. When I walked in on the first day, everybody looked at me as though I was an alien from another planet, civilization, whatever . . . And then I saw Josie. We spotted each other immediately. Like me, Josie was wearing interesting black clothes that matched her long, dark, straight hair. She looked brilliant, like a vampire!

From that very first day we hung out together. She was brilliant, smart, funny and she got all the best marks for essays and projects, but I was better at art than her. I almost wished I wasn't because it seemed like nothing and no one could prove to Josie how good she was – she'd never believe them, not even the teachers when they asked her to apply to Oxford and Cambridge; she just laughed. "Can you imagine me there?"

I could, but she couldn't. I knew I was going to Art School when I finished my exams and Josie said she would apply to college in the same town so we could share a flat and have fun. We certainly never intended to stay in the country. We had a game plan, and we were going to stick to it.

It was so great to have someone to hang out with, and she knew where all the best music places were in town, all the record shops and pubs where bands played. She was brilliant with a sewing machine, so we'd make fantastic witch-like costumes to haunt the streets in. Of course the locals didn't always appreciate our unique creativity, how could they? So we were often on the wrong end of a witch hunt, a bit like that crazy film *The Wicker Man*. But all these adversities made the glue stronger between the two of us. Us against the heathens!

Josie never invited me home to her place, she'd always stay at mine, until one day there was a gig in the town she lived in, so I took the bus over. Her parents were very odd, that's all I can say. They were like two people who were living in an alternative time. They weren't even that old but they dressed as if they were grandparents to Josie rather than her mum and dad. They had tea at four, with sandwiches and cakes. Everything in the house was very old-fashioned (even the television looked like it came from the 1970s) and tidier than tidy, except in Josie's room. And they treated Josie as if she was one of the china tea cups in their tea set. They wanted to know everything about what we got up to and obviously we couldn't tell them everything – they would have died of a heart attack – so Josie lied a lot. They weren't little lies either, they were mountains. I wouldn't be able to remember all those lies but Josie was very clever, and she thought it was funny. I had begun to notice it was really weird stuff that seemed to make her laugh.

When it came to filling in our forms for uni, I was applying for Art School, and I saw that Josie was doing the same. I couldn't understand why she wasn't applying to do English because she was brilliant at that, but she said she wanted to go to the same place as me. Well, of course I wanted that too – she was my best friend – but if I was being honest, I didn't think she'd get in because when it came to art she was always copying other people's ideas.

Two weeks before my interview for Art School, disaster struck. My portfolio disappeared from the art room. Josie and I searched the whole college, from top to toe, and when I collapsed in tears because I couldn't find it, she comforted me and made me believe that I'd be able to do enough new work to get through it all. She was great at seeing me through the crisis, bringing me little presents and making me cards to cheer me up.

College wasn't very helpful, but Mum and Dad were great in any disaster – they knew how to pull together. They cleared the sitting room and gave it over to me for the next two weeks and I worked like crazy. Some of what I did was even better than my old stuff. I went to stay with my brother the night before the interview. Josie's parents were taking her down the next day. I got my appointment mixed up, and arrived two hours early, at eleven instead of one, but I sat and waited and tried not to get too nervous. Josie had told me her interview was the last one, at six o'clock, and I'd miss her, but as I sat there she walked out of the interview room.

Of course she saw me and looked as startled as a cat being chased by a dog. She looked down immediately to what she was carrying in her hand and my eyes followed her shifty gaze. She was holding my portfolio.

I couldn't believe, I still can't, that my best friend had stolen my work to get into the same college as me. Maybe I'd be able to understand it if she wasn't good at anything else, but she was.

As it was, I got in and she didn't. Divine retribution? Maybe. Maybe she did me a favour. Having to do all that new work focused me, made me really think about what I wanted to do in art. I was angry, really angry for a long while and I couldn't talk to her. There was nothing she could have said that would have explained or made reasonable what she did. Now I just feel sorry for her, it seems such a waste. I thought we were the same and we obviously never were. I think I just wanted to believe that we were because we liked the same clothes; how shallow can you get?

She's still in the country – I heard she's engaged to some bloke she works with in the pub by college. Me? I'm in the city, starting my second year at Art School, and I'm sharing a flat with three boys and we're

making a film together. Maybe sometimes bad things
work out for the best.

A Tale of Two Peters

Karen O – lead singer-songwriter of US pop group the Yeah Yeah Yeahs
yeahyeahyeahs.com

I was born in Seoul, Korea – my Mum's Korean and my Dad's Polish-American – but I grew up in Bergin County, New Jersey, about thirty minutes from New York City. We moved to the USA when I was two, and I was fourteen when I met Peter. He was six feet six inches tall, with a big nose, red hair and he had a hunched back from always stooping.

I went to the same private schools with the same kids from junior into high school. For some reason there was a bunch of new kids who arrived when we were all fourteen, and I guess I befriended Peter because he was a novelty, but also because I had a messed-up relationship with my elder brother.

My brother and I had got on when we were younger, but after that we fought all the time because I was the baby of the family. I think I was drawn to Peter subconsciously, as a replacement for the relationship I didn't have with my brother. I mean, we were the same age, but because he was so big, and because he had the same awkward, lonely, nerdy thing going on as my brother, there was a similarity, but Peter also had this super-dry sense of humour. He would really crack me up. I hardly ever acknowledge it, but he was also my first formative influence in music. He was a singer and songwriter, had taught himself how to play guitar and wrote these acoustic songs, kind of like Neil Young. He loved Neil Young but I didn't even have a clue who Neil Young was.

Peter would give me tapes all the time, of his songs that he'd recorded himself. I remember one went:

> *My mind is twisted*
> *Around the thought of you*
> *I'm so glad you missed it*
> *When I said I loved you.*

I was really young then, and totally obsessed with falling in love with someone, but I never realised that it could be with Peter. I mean Peter and I were best friends, we talked all the time at school, on the phone, back and forth, back and forth.

Then suddenly, without telling me, in Tenth Grade he got a nose job because he had this huge nose. He said he had to have it done because he had something wrong with his septum, but I didn't believe him. He looked really weird without his real nose, but what was REALLY weird, was that it was the beginning of his transformation.

Peter had always had this harum of sycophants, a bunch of dorky kids who were fixated with him, because although he was this red-headed, geeky giant, he was always really charismatic. But after the operation, he began to change his personality too. He started to get really cocky. So as usual I made fun of him, teased him, pushed his buttons. I remember I said, "Oh, Peter you never write songs about me." So he wrote this song about me which started:

> *Oh, Karen,*
> *So cold and barren . . .*

He had really hurt my feelings, and I told him, so he wrote another song for me, which wasn't half as good and was all syrupy and kinda went:

> *Hey, Karen, I'd stop caring,*
> *Karen's eyes are . . .*

Then one day he rang me up, and just started shouting down the phone at me, "Karen, you're a bitch. I don't have to hang out with people like you in my life."

And he stopped talking to me, cut me off. He wouldn't even acknowledge me at school. That was it. Then Peter dropped all of us from school, he'd only hang out with the posh, waspy kids from the super white high school in the next town.

I cried myself to sleep for the whole of that junior year, every night. Peter's personality had changed so dramatically as if he was way 'too cool for school'. He dressed differently and wouldn't talk to any of his old friends, and the real cherry on top was when the Battle of the Bands happened at school. It's like this competition where everybody performs. So Peter performed, 'Sexual Healing' by Marvin Gaye, and he was trying to be all sexy and stuff, like he was boasting. I don't know maybe he was seeing some girl or something. My heart was broken into a billion pieces and it was all I could think of or talk about. I felt totally lost.

I remember in senior year he called me, totally out of the blue. I'd been off school for a couple of weeks with the flu and he apologised for not speaking to me for so long, but he was still really bitter, and he wouldn't tell me what about. He just said he didn't want to talk about it. I told him, "I've been really hurting, Peter," and he was totally unsympathetic. It was like a dream. There was so much distance between us. It was like talking to an empty shell, a ghost. Then I began to think that I didn't know him at all, he didn't want to be anything like that old Peter. He'd killed him dead. He'd lost his humour, he was just cold and cool, and there was no sweetness left.

Oh man, it was weird. And even his music started to suck. I listened to those tapes he'd given me over and over again, trying to work out what had happened. It was so weird, because we'd never even held hands, it was totally platonic between us, but I'd never felt heartbroken before; I was bereft.

Peter dropped all his friends, even James who he used to write music with. James also drew comics and he started drawing all these pictures of Peter: Peter and the Aliens. The Aliens had kidnapped him in a spaceship and he was trying to wave at us, but in his place, the Aliens had left a clone Peter. We used to joke that somewhere, far away, still existed, the real Peter.

I met him again when I was nineteen, and he looked so different, his face and neck thick-set and unattractive. He used to be super skinny and gawky cute, when he was young. He told me that his elder bipolar brother, who was his guitar hero, had been on a bunch of medication and had jumped in front of a train trying to commit suicide. He didn't die, just lost an arm so he couldn't play the guitar any more. He got ill and then just kinda died. I knew Peter had a rough time with his family but he didn't share what was going on. He still treated me as if I had done something unforgiveable, but never divulged what it was. After that meeting he seemed so weird, for a time I was worried that he'd try and kill me or something.

I had a really strange, warped sensibility when it came to men after all that Peter stuff. I was shattered, totally distrustful.

Yet when I went to art college in Ohio, the first guy I befriended was a small, red-headed guy called Peter. He restored my faith in men, he was so totally sweet, happy and loving. Unconditionally loving, but he had this really twisted funny sense of humour. He was loyal too. When everyone at Ohio turned against me after I'd broken up with some boy and everybody was bad-mouthing me, he said he didn't care what people said, it was an irritation, like a small buzzing in his ear.

We wrote songs together, played music, made films, were room mates. Some of my happiest times were when we both transferred to NYU film school and he used to come over to my apartment on Avenue A and we'd play the purest music, singing our hearts out, our voices completely complimentary:

> *I'm not sorry . . . when it's starry,*
> *'Cos I keep trippin'.*

And we'd be singing and the downstairs neighbour would be banging on her ceiling with a broom, telling us to keep the noise down and we'd keep on singing and laughing.

He was this great guy.

After university ended, we were all miserable and bored. I was doing the Yeah Yeah Yeahs and I guess Peter and I weren't seeing as much of each other since he'd started with this girlfriend who was always depressed; she was a real soul-sucker. Nobody thought Peter was depressed but he was doing odd things like getting drunk in the middle of the day and, taking his girlfriend's medication. I mean, we all used to get drunk but nobody thought he'd kill himself.

Neither of us had jobs at the time. It was a weekday and our friends were all working. There was a new planetarium that had opened in the National History Museum and we agreed to go together, the next day. In the morning I called him but it went onto answer-phone, so I was shouting trying to wake him up. I left a load of these obnoxious rude messages, and finally I gave up and decided to go by myself.

I was wearing my headphones listening to this song over and over by Nick in the band, called 'Procession'. I felt strangely good that day. I began to notice things about people on the subway, intricate little things that I wouldn't normally, and I wrote them all down in my notebook I was carrying. In the museum there were all these groups of little kids running about and old people, it was like a zoo of families, and I sat and drew them, then went into the planetarium. I was lying back with my headphones on full listening to Nick's song on repeat looking at the heavens, feeling super-connected with the universe. I was thinking, "I feel so good – I'm going to get off medication" – I'd been taking pills for anxiety attacks since I was twenty.

When I got home at the end of the day, there were

all these messages on my cellphone – "Karen call me, it's an emergency." I called and Peter was dead. Immediately I said, "How? Did he get hit by a car?" I couldn't believe it.

He had hung himself with a tie from some exercise bars for his girlfriend to see as soon as she walked into the apartment. He left no suicide note. I think he must have been dead already when I was leaving all those awful messages.

Everybody, all his friends were convening downtown. It was raining, I grabbed a cab. I was still listening to the same song I'd been listening to all day. I sat there and I knew Peter took the ride with me, held my hand. I had such a pure feeling of redemption, it was one of the most poetic and beautiful days of my life. Magical and unbelievable.

It was 21 February 2001; in September later that year the twin towers would be crashed. Peter's death must have affected a hundred people close to him. I was already suffering from a blanket of grief and then all the people who died on 11 September turned New York upside down – the impact of all those deaths was like an atom bomb on all those tens of thousands of people.

I cringe when I meet a Peter now. I'm dreadfully superstitious – 2001 was the year of the Rat, and Rats are always bad news for Horses. I don't have any red-headed male friends anymore, either. I couldn't even go to Peter's funeral, I couldn't bear to see him going into a grave. I'd always been so obsessed by death and dying, but this was my first big loss.

Sure you grieve any break-up. There is no consolation for missing Peter, not in this lifetime. It is more jarring to have had him disappear than seeing the first Peter metamorphose into someone else. You know, it doesn't make sense to me still.

Do You Believe in Telepathy?

Becky, 15

Gemma is my only best friend. She will always be my best friend, even if we never speak again.

I knew the very first time I saw her that we were going to be best friends. I can't explain why, I just knew. It was kind of spooky and Gemma said she felt exactly the same. Maybe we're psychic or telepathic or something.

It was weird because I'd never had a 'one and only' best friend before. I guess I've always had lots of friends. I like them, but I also like being by myself, if that makes sense? I like being alone and not having to talk, or just lying on the grass looking up at the sky and thinking. I know it might seem boring to some people, but I like it. I'm not one of those desperate friends that need a lot of time and effort and are always running around spilling out their problems, crying and having fits. I suppose I prefer to be a little private. It's just the way I am. I like things to be easy and fun. I'd never be jealous or possessive – I don't understand thinking that you can own someone, that's why it was so strange meeting Gemma, and just knowing.

Gemma was unpacking a suitcase when I first saw her. She had just arrived at boarding school, two weeks later than everyone else. I didn't know why at the time. I walked into the dormitory and she was taking all these amazing clothes from New York and Paris and London out of her enormous trunk, beautiful clothes in lovely colours and materials. I asked if I could help her and we started to talk, about where she got all the clothes from and how her parents were both fashion designers so she got loads of free clothes. She called them samples. This seemed funny at the time, because at the doctor I'd been asked to give a 'sample' of my pee, for some test.

We made each other laugh straightaway, joked around, and when we'd finished unpacking we walked around the school and the grounds. I showed her everything I had learned about the place, and then we went to high tea together. By then we knew that we liked the same bands, the same clothes, movies, books, even the same food, and dancing. We both love dancing. We are the same height, though I've got light brown hair, almost blond, and Gemma has red hair. She's very pale and pretty.

In fact Gemma is a year older than me – but it didn't matter.

I really think the last two years have been the best of my whole life. I've never laughed so much. You know that kind of laughing that has you rolling around on the floor, and you just can't help yourself, you can't breath and your sides are left aching from it. That belly-aching laughing that seizes you. Giggling that doesn't stop, and really irritates grown-ups, and *still* doesn't stop, even when they start shouting at you, which just makes you want to laugh more and more. That's what it's been like getting to know Gemma – hilarious. The stories she told me about her family, you just wouldn't believe.

I'd never been 'popular' before, but for almost two years Gemma and I were the most popular girls in the whole school. Every day was fun and most people can't say that about school, but then most people don't get to have a friend like Gemma, ever.

The only time we spent apart was during lessons, because she was in the year above me. Otherwise we brushed our teeth together, took showers together, got dressed and ate breakfast together, spent break times together, and every day after school until Prep. After doing our homework we'd have cocoa together, around the big roaring fire in the winter. Of course we weren't always alone, most of the time our other friends were with us, but we were never far apart, and we would share the humour of a situation with our eyes. We didn't have a secret language that we needed to make up and speak, we could communicate without speaking. We seemed to know just what the other was thinking. I don't know how it worked, but it did. Spooky!

We shared everything: our clothes, shoes, make-up and toiletries, and even had our periods at the same time. Since we were also the same bra size, we could share those too. We even once swapped boyfriends, as a joke, with boys we just occasionally got off with for a snog at parties or discos. Boys weren't really the point, but they were good to talk about, especially after lights-out at night. Luckily, we never fancied the same boys. We agreed on everything. I know that sounds boring but it wasn't, because we were always discussing important things too – like our joint sense of ambition, sense of humour, and sense of injustice about the world, like famine and war. We spent time together because we had fun, even if we were just walking to the village to buy sweets.

There is nothing I would change about the last two years, except the last week of term before we broke up for Easter. But there was really nothing I could do about what happened. I'd like to blame someone for taking Gemma away, but I can't blame Gemma, and I don't even know whose fault it was.

Separated during lessons we sat with other friends. I always sat next to Julio, a Spanish day boy who can't speak English very well, but it didn't matter, because he drew these fantastic cartoons and we'd swap pictures with each other. He's really good at maths and helped me, and I helped him with English. Julio is the only person apart from the teachers who still speaks to me. I expect I'll spend most of the rest of the year in the library with no one talking to me, which is all right, because I've got exams coming up. I mean who needs friends when you've got revision!

Mary-Jane and Lizzie sat on either side of Gemma. They were always trying to get her away to do things by themselves, without me. I didn't mind – not that much, anyway – because those were times I could be alone and go and write poetry and think. Anyway, I couldn't blame anyone for wanting to be Gemma's friend, she had something that everybody wanted but you couldn't work out what it was. It was a kind of energy, life, fun. The thing that makes a room full of people suddenly become a party. She has this confidence and a belief that everything is going to work out for the best, and when she tells you, you can believe it too. You want to be the best you can with her, funny and the cleverest you've ever been.

Usually as soon as the bell went we would find each other like magnets or like heat-seeking missiles, and we'd go off to walk and talk about everything: the good things and the bad stuff that had happened during the day. Chewing over it all like it was a bone. Gemma has this really horrible stepfather that hits her and her brother. The whole of the house is carpeted in white and if he finds any dirt anywhere he hunts them down and beats them. Putting it like that makes it sound scary and cruel, which it is, but the way she tells the stories they always come out funny. Only Gemma could make being hit sound funny.

It was a Saturday, and morning school had just finished. Usually Gemma and I would hook up and have lunch, but I couldn't find her. She had been going off with the others more recently, so I went to read in the common room. When some of the young kids burst in and put the TV on I left and walked towards the cricket pavilion. The weather wasn't that nice and I don't know what made me go there, I don't usually. Now I wonder if it was telepathy. I didn't notice that there were people there, I couldn't hear them and I was reading as I walked – a very bad habit, I know, because I always trip over things. As I entered the pavilion I tripped over the legs of a boy called Bean, and then I saw Mary-Jane and Lizzie, Tony and Josh, and on the floor was a bottle of pills, and some bottles of vodka. And then I saw Gemma, collapsed in a heap. All of them were completely zoned out. I tried to talk, to shake Gemma, get her to talk back, but there was nothing there but a faraway smile. I couldn't carry her and she couldn't walk, she couldn't even open her eyes. I had to leave her.

I dropped my book, picked up the bottle and ran as

fast as I could back to school and the main house for help. I didn't know what to do. I ran into the flat belonging to the girls' housemistress, Mrs Brian, and shrieked out everything and gave her the empty pill bottle. Mrs Brian rang the boys' housemaster and the Head and they phoned for an ambulance. Then they took a Land Rover down to the games pitch. The ambulance arrived as they came back. I watched everything from Mrs Brian's window, she sat me down and made me a cup of tea with lots of sugar in it. She told me to drink it, to stop me from crying, but I couldn't. I knew they'd all be in really bad trouble and my stomach churned with the thought of it. I felt sick and empty and sad, all at the same time. I knew I had betrayed Gemma.

Mrs Brian and the Head both said I'd done the right thing, but I still feel bad, nothing they can say changes that. They're all being expelled, but are allowed to come back just to take their exams. All but Gemma, who, they said, had had problems at her last school with lying. Basically she'd been expelled from there, too, which was why she'd arrived later than the rest of us. So Gemma's not coming back, ever. Of course she had problems! But what am I supposed to do? Tell on Gemma again to the Head, explain how her stepfather beats her? How he'll kill her if she goes home? But what if everything she told me was a lie?

Was it Gemma who got all that lot to take the pills

with her? Was it Mary-Jane's fault for stealing her grandmother's pills, or her grandmother's for leaving them lying about? Or was it my fault for telling the housemistress?

I don't know why I feel so confused about it all. If I hadn't told, someone might have died. But in the last week of school nobody talked to me. Every time anyone passed me they'd hiss and whisper, "Grass" or "Snitch"; they laugh at me in corners, point and sneer. I don't know what's going to happen next term, I'm dreading it because it's the summer term and the longest one and I've got to do exams which means I can't even leave. I'm frightened.

I try to rationalise it. I don't know what else I could have done in the circumstances. I hope she understands one day. I was trying to save Gemma, my best friend, but all I've done is lose her. I've lost my very best friend in the world and I don't know if I'll ever find her again. And being alone, it's just not the same, I don't care what anybody says. This whole thing is like a nightmare and nobody seems to understand, not even my mum, and usually she does. It's just so horrible being me and being stuck there. And the worse thing is, I don't think I can ever trust myself to feel the same way about anything anymore. Not after this.

SMITH AND ME

RUBY, 16

We met at school, aged six, and we were the only two in the class with glasses. The only differences between us were that I had long hair worn in two plaits down my back, and my glasses had a sticky mess of fleshy pink fabric plaster over one lens and his didn't. But we both had fringes, and we were the same height, size and colouring.

It was not until we met in the square that we began to be real friends. Cautiously at first – after all, he was a boy and I was a girl. But over the months of summer in our eighth year we stopped letting that get between us. Maybe it was the glasses that made us get on so well?

The other girls and boys in the square, along with my sisters, teased Smith and me about our friendship. They said Smith was my boyfriend. But he wasn't. He was my friend, best friend.

Sometimes we were embarrassed enough to return to our single sex armies. We were never apart that long because in the end it was really only Smith that

I got on with. How could I pretend to enjoy dolls' tea parties, makeovers and beauty treatments when my favourite garment was a pair of blue overalls with specific places for keeping spanners, hammers and other essentials? I was a real tomboy. I didn't mind the thought of mud face packs, but I preferred applying them fresh from the flowerbed in a single, swift hand movement to another little girl's face who was getting on my nerves. Other girls irritated me – I had enough of them at home with three sisters.

I think Smith's parents thought it a little strange that whenever we had sleepovers it was just each other we invited. Mrs Smith wouldn't allow it after we turned ten – no matter how fond she was of me – she declared it 'unnatural'. Things began to change anyway, by the end of our tenth summer. In future, if I was to stay over I had to sleep in the spare room, alone. There was to be no discussion, no matter how spooky their house was at night. It took the fun out of it. Then he wasn't allowed over to our house by his mother. I think she thought there were too many women there, even before my father left. My mum said she was overprotective; I suppose she was right.

They lived in a huge old Victorian house on the corner of our square. It was far too big for them, Mum said, with Smith's brother Peter away at school. Smith's real name was John but there were too many other Johns at school and the teacher had decided to avoid confusion by calling John by his last name, Smith.

There was the whole of his house and mine around the corner, but we always preferred the square in the middle: our territory. Whether it was cold and rainy, or hot and muggy, we could make hideouts and as much noise as we liked without being afraid of being told off. We turned the climbing frame into a pirates' ship, sometimes we sailed it as though it were a galleon ship on the high seas, leaving furious pirates in our wake. Or it was a great big dinosaur and we were prehistoric hunters, or a spaceship and we were off to another galaxy. Occasionally it metamorphosed into a steam engine that had to be fixed before it took a precious cargo of bullion across the Wild West. Sometimes, the natives would attack and great battles ensued, or sometimes it was the cowboys – whoever it was, we always had a battle on our hands.

We got many ideas for games from old films – *Batman* was my favourite. I would alternate between being Catwoman and Robin, depending on the story we'd invented. Smith was always Batman.

Often unsuspecting strangers, having picnics on the grass in the summer, or walking their dogs through the soggy leaves on a wet autumn day, played the parts of unsuspecting baddies. In our minds we tied them up and had them locked away in jails or thrown down canyons, and all the time they remained innocently unaware of their roles as cat-strangling dog-eaters.

All it took was for one of us to say, "Holy moly, Batman," and we were driving along in the Batmobile.

"Holy moly, Batman."

"I know, Robin. It's hard to imagine there are people as evil as that nanny with the green pram. We will have to rescue the stolen baby, before she escapes from the gardens."

"Good idea."

"Block all exits."

"Done. Trip wire and explosive bugs in place."

"What are these damned children doing messing around with the gates? I don't think they should be allowed in the square unaccompanied." The nurse was speaking to another passing Nazi spy.

The next moment we were lost in space, orbiting around Mars before landing on a strange planet, either of us changing destinations at the click of a finger, with the other loyally following.

We giggled all the time – my mum called us the Giggle Twins. We could be anyone we chose and yet the adult world couldn't see our invisible disguises. To them we looked like children, just normal children. A boy and a girl, odd little Bod-like creatures who both wore glasses.

Then my family and I went on holiday for the whole of the summer. I hadn't seen Smith for weeks and weeks but when we got back it poured for three days solid and by the time I made it out to the square, the summer was ending and Smith was nowhere. I didn't dare ring on his bell, his mother was a scary sort of woman who I felt didn't like me, or didn't approve of me playing with her son. Then, just when I'd given up hope and assumed they'd sent him away to an orphanage, I saw him from the climbing frame. I was hanging upside down pretending to be a monkey in the jungle, a little sad when you're alone and twelve. It was definitely Smith, in a new school uniform. I shrieked and almost fell off the top rung as I clambered down. "Smith! Smith," I cried. "It's me. Ruby." I was running to the gate.

"Hello, Ruby." He spoke in a very un-Smith-like manner, hardly moving his mouth at all. "I'm at Grayson Prep now." His face was all closed up, his eyes like a gated community.

"Is that a boarding school?" I felt so childish next to him in his smart, grey flannel suit with long trousers; stupid and babyish in my trainers and muddy jeans.

"Oh no. It's just Mother says she doesn't like me going in the square now, I have so much work to do. Homework."

"Bad luck."

He scuffed his toe against the pavement and looked sheepishly downwards, before looking at me through his long lashes and glasses. His expression was a mixture of regret and sadness. "Sorry, Rube." For a moment, that moment I had him back.

"It's not your fault." I somehow already knew what he was going to say.

"Mother said if I do well in my exams I can go out." He looked at me as if wondering whether I could deal with the truth, or did I have to be fobbed off with some lie. "Mother thinks I should be friends with boys, Ruby. I shouldn't only have a girl as a friend. She says it's not normal."

I nodded my head, my eyes fixed on his brand new shoes that were like his father's, black and shiny with laces. We were powerless, however much we wanted things to be different. There was nothing we could do that would change the situation. He was a boy and I was a girl, and it wasn't normal, his mum said, and the onlookers in the square had always seemed to agree. I'd heard their comments, how unusual it was, a girl playing like a boy. Why couldn't I play with the girls and why would a boy want to play with a girl unless he was gay. As if being gay was bad.

There was nothing I could say except, "I'll make special prayers."

"Yes, do." Smith closed his eyes and bit his lip just like when we used to hold hands and wish together, in our own world. I could hear his mother calling his name. "I've got to go now."

"See ya. Wouldn't want to be ya." It was our usual language, and I was trying to make light of my great loss. I bit my lip so hard I could feel the blood rushing to it, I had to do something to stop the pain in my throat and my eyes filling. I didn't want to cry.

"Me neither," he murmured. He made a small wave back, scrunching up his eyes and freckled nose against the sun and blinking his eyes as slowly as a cat. When he opened them he'd returned to their world, and me to mine. Before he had reached his doorstep, I had turned away, running, lying, pretending that Smith meant nothing, that our friendship for all those years was as easily disposed of and forgotten as an empty can of Coke.

I still miss him. It's something I find hard to explain. I mean, I still see him about our neighbourhood and even at parties, but he isn't Smith any longer. I suppose what I miss is how it was between us. That's gone. What I want to know is, why can't you continue to be best friends like that with boys when you're a teenager? Why do we have to get older and spoil things?

Taking Chances

Charlotte Cooper – bass guitarist, The Subways
www.thesubways.net

I didn't have any really close friends at school. I was always quiet and very shy. I had friends at my competitive swimming club, which was where I met my boyfriend Billy (lead guitarist and singer of The Subways) and his brother, Josh (our drummer). It was funny, none of us had close friendships at school – I wonder if that's why we swam? Or maybe it was because we were training four times a week after school, and three times a week before school started in the mornings.

I had friends at school to talk to, but no one I would have called my best friend, no soul mate sort of thing – I knew who Ally was, saw her about – she was very beautiful, popular, always laughing. I used to think that if one day we ever did start to talk, she was the kind of girl that I could be really good friends with. In the way that lots of girls these days feel about Kate Moss or Paris Hilton, I suppose. You look at somebody, even if it's a picture, and you identify with them, yet you don't know them. It usually happens to famous people, like the Julia Roberts character in *Notting Hill*, one of my favourite films.

I was in Year Ten of my mixed comprehensive school in Essex, aged fourteen or fifteen, when a German exchange programme was put up on the notice board at school. I always really liked German, so I applied by myself, even though I was nervous and shy about not knowing anyone else on the trip. Later I discovered that most of the people on the trip were boys, the only other girl going in my year was Ally.

We sat together on the plane and really chatted for the first time. It was great because she'd lived in Germany before, so she was able to tell me all these things about a country I'd never been to, and a language and people I didn't know. But we were both really anxious about what kind of families we were going to be staying with – apart from a few letters exchanged with our German pen-pals we didn't have a clue what these strangers were going to be like. The one thing that comforted us was knowing that we'd be getting together during the day with the rest of our English schoolmates to go sightseeing, or go to the German schools around Nuremburg.

German food was so different, even breakfast, and you never wear outdoor shoes in the home – you have to put on special house shoes. It was a different lifestyle from what we were used to. Staying with a family seemed odd, not knowing if I could say I was hungry outside of meals, tired when it wasn't bedtime, trying to be polite, but suddenly I had Ally to talk it over with each day when we got together, and that made the whole experience less stressful, more fun. We laughed a lot about all the German stuff, but everything else too. What I liked about her, still like about her, is that she's very open, non-judgemental. From the start, there were lots of things that we had in common. We both like loads of different types of music, and we're both naturally cat people and love Audrey Hepburn, but also there's also lots that we don't have in common. I have one sister Louise who's two years younger than me; Ally has five brothers and sisters. My mum and dad are still married, Ally has a stepfather.

I know why I like Ally – she's great fun to be around, enjoys making new friends and experiencing new things, and apart from her being so supportive, she has made me feel a lot more confident about myself. I mean Billy does that too, and obviously being on stage makes you feel confident, but Ally has also contributed to me feeling good about myself, less self-conscious. I don't know why you click with some people but not with others. We've been close ever since.

I was already going out with Billy and playing in the band, mostly local gigs, when I met Ally, but since then she has always come along to our gigs to support us. In those early years not many people apart from Ally and teachers, whose classes I had to cut early, knew that I was leaving to go to London to play gigs. Billy is very particular about who he likes to talk to, but he likes Ally and she likes him; they get along great.

Ally and I did A-level German and Philosophy together, so we saw each other regularly at school. In those two years I also had a job, school work and the band. I needed the job to help pay for train fares as the gigs didn't cover all our costs. We both had boyfriends who weren't at our school, but it has always been different with Billy and me. We've been solid from when we first met, aged fourteen. He asked me to join the band, suggested I learn bass and we really learned our instruments together. Ally's had more up-and-down relationships. Of course, once you finish school it becomes harder to sustain any relationships, friends drop away as you all go off to do different things, but Billy and I are in the band.

I thought about going to university like Ally, but then I realised that actually music was now my full-time job – I didn't need to do anything else. We had our first album come out in Britain and America, 'Young for Eternity', and we toured the States. It was very exciting. In the last year we've played Japan, Australia and New Zealand, and Europe. The music world is very male and journalists are always asking me if I think it's sexist, but to be honest although most of the time I'm the only girl in the room, I don't notice or feel myself to be any different from the boys. However, I feel it's important for me to see Ally whenever I can, catch up with my girl friend.

Since we've been touring the world so much in the last year I make the time to contact her even if it's only for a cup of coffee. I see the strain that being away for long periods of time puts upon relationships, friends aren't always going to want to wait around. Real friends like Ally, that I have a proper connection with are different. You go away, haven't seen them for ages, and when you see them again and talk, it's like you've never been away and you know you've got something special. I certainly miss her when I'm away, but we talk on the phone and text each other all the time. When we play London, now that Ally's doing journalism at university, she brings along all her new friends so I get to meet them all. I haven't hung out with her at her uni bar, but it's something I'd really like to do. I've invited her along to photo shoots and I've introduced her to people on magazines so she's got some work experience out of it. Friendships are about helping each other, and she's always helped me.

Meeting Ally was a big lesson to me: I'd taken a chance to do something on my own and I made a fantastic friend on the way. You never know who you are going to meet or where. I try now to talk to as many people as I can, because they can tell you about their different lives and experiences. If you're just wrapped up in your shyness and stay home in front of the telly, who are you going to meet? What are you going to do with your life? Sometimes you have to be brave enough to talk to the people that you admire, just like I did with Ally.

In the future I see us still being friends, maybe with husbands and kids; it's a long way off. Already I've been playing in The Subways for five years and I'm nineteen. It's only a little bit longer than I've had Ally as my best friend. Each morning I wake up with a sense of excitement, I want to play an instrument, write a song or play a gig, and Ally has that same enthusiasm for life. It's when you know that what you're doing is entirely right, whether you're being a mother or working in a shop, you have to love it to be good at something. I can't imagine myself not doing my music and playing in The Subways, in the same way, that I can't really imagine not having Ally as my best friend.

Rare

Katrina, 14

I see my cousins every summer holiday. I mean, I *used* to see them every summer holiday. I would always go and stay with them. Sometimes if my mum could get time off work she'd come too, for a week or so, but I always went for the whole of the summer. Auntie Janie and Uncle Dennis live by the sea in this lovely little town. It's practically like my other home, I know it so well. My cousins are called Sim (short for Simeon), who's ten, and Jake, who's eight, and until last year there was Kate.

Together Kate and I were the 2K's, and because we were the only girls we spent all our time together. We even kind of looked alike with our dark curly hair and brown eyes; we had the same dimple, only one and on our left cheeks. She'd introduce me sometimes as her honorary sis.

When we were younger she always treated me like I was a bit of a baby – which was ridiculous, because I was only nine months younger than she was – but as we got older the age gap made no difference.

Sometimes to tease me she'd say in the middle of one of our intense conversations (we were always having intense conversations), "I always forget that you're so much younger than me, because sometimes you can be quite intelligent. Must be because you're a Kat. A Kitkat." If she was a normal friend I would have jumped on her, but Kate always managed to get away with murder. I would have to content myself with a "Ha bloody ha".

Whenever we left the house, Auntie Janie had this way of sticking her head around the door and saying, "Oh, Katrina, make sure you look after my Kate." And she'd smile in this not very happy way. But then Auntie Janie *wasn't* very happy; she was always a little anxious because Kate had been born with a hole in her heart that the doctors had not been able to fix. They said there was a chance they might be able to do something when she was older or it might even get better by itself, but meanwhile, I had to look after her.

Kate wasn't allowed to run, jump, get too excited or play sport other than the odd game of mini golf. Not that I liked sport, but I wouldn't have minded a go on the big dipper or log flume at the fair occasionally. She always said, "Oh, go on it, Kat! Go on, have a go. I don't care if you want to throw up everywhere." She'd even try to give me the money, but I wouldn't – it wouldn't be fair to Kate to do something she couldn't do. Sometimes we'd mooch about the fair, laughing at people being spun around, turned upside down and being bumped by the dodgems until their candy floss and hot dog dinners returned over the tarmac. Yes, Kate used to think that was very funny.

On hot days in the heat of the summer, we would lie all day on the beach, swapping fantasies about our future lives and who would fall in love with us. We'd swim in the bay, where we'd once seen a dolphin, we were always looking out for him again. I don't know why we thought it was a him, it might have been a girl. In the winter, we'd walk about town, get chips from Gerry's fish shop, and if it was raining we'd sit under the pier and watch the waves crashing. Other times we liked going to jumble sales on Saturdays and buying hideous things and cutting them apart and making them into some 'bad' skirt or dress.

The thing was, we just always got on, we were never bored. I suppose, looking back, we took each other for granted. We made no effort to keep in touch during term time, because we always knew we'd see each other as soon as the holidays came around again. We always said we'd send e-mails or texts but we never kept it up. I don't know why, except that we had our other lives, our own lives. And Kate's best friend at school always went away during the holidays, so maybe I was like her stand-in, or she was mine. Anyhow, Kate didn't have loads of friends. People thought she was a bit weird because she wore wild clothes and she wasn't like the other townie trendy girls, but that was just Kate. In a city it wouldn't have made any difference, but at the seaside, everybody likes to look and behave the same, nice and normal.

It was last summer that everything went wrong. It was a warm day with just the right amount of breeze and we were swimming in the bay. The sun jumping off the ripples of waves; picture perfect. One of those really lovely, clear blue sky days, the sun shining down pure and strong enough to make you believe the sea wouldn't be that cold, though it always was freezing until you got used to it. We were just swimming, and floating on our backs. Then Kate found something really disgusting in the water – and she threw it on to me and I screamed. I was hysterical when I saw it because I thought it was human poo, from the sewage pipe – actually it was just rotting wood. Kate started laughing and she couldn't stop and whilst I went underwater to try and wash off what I thought was poo, she kept laughing. When I surfaced, Kate had disappeared, I dived down into the water, and I couldn't see her and I kept diving down and I found her arm and I pulled her up to the surface and I tried to swim her to shore, and then a man came along and helped me. We tried to give her the kiss of life, over and over again, but nothing happened. Someone called the ambulance and they tried the same, and then they took her in the ambulance and I ran back to the house to find Auntie Janie to tell her, but she wasn't in. No one was in, so I called Mum and I was crying so much she couldn't understand what I was saying, and I was trying to tell her that Kate had drowned and that I had tried to save her, but she couldn't understand what I was saying because of all my crying. I couldn't stop. She made me wait on the phone while she called Uncle Dennis at work and then she made me say it all over again, about hospital and the ambulance. Later, we went up to the hospital. Auntie Janie came back with the boys and we drove up there. I tried to tell Auntie about how it had happened and everything, but she wouldn't look at me, she wouldn't say a thing to me – it was as though I wasn't there. Mum drove down and picked me up the next day. Auntie Janie wouldn't say goodbye. She couldn't look at me; she still can't.

The doctor said that I had been brilliant in the circumstances, that there was nothing else I could have done, that Kate's heart was the trouble – it had gone before she drowned. Mum says I've got to stop blaming myself, and I don't blame myself, but I know Auntie Janie blames me. She said to Mum that she would rather I didn't come down and visit any more. She didn't even want Mum or me at Kate's funeral. She said to Mum that she finds it too hard to look at me, now that Kate's not here any more. But I don't just miss Kate, I miss Auntie Janie too. And I miss Sim and

Jake and I don't know if I'll ever see them again. But most of all I miss Kate. Mum says give it time, but it's been a year, and time can't change what happened – how can it?

At home it's just me and Mum. I love Mum and everything, and I love it being just us two. It's so much nicer than when Dad was about, always screaming and shouting and getting violent. When he did still live with us, it was great escaping in the summer to be with a normal family and Kate. Mum has to work a lot and there's never that smell of cooking and a table crammed full of food and home-baked cakes for tea. When I was little, when Dad was still around, I used to pray at night for Auntie Janie and Uncle Dennis to adopt me. Now it feels like a whole part of my life has disappeared, and there's nothing I can do to bring it back. Nothing.

It's been a whole year since she died and it's so weird. I still think I see her, walking down the street, but it's not a street she'd ever walked down. It's strange because I really think it's her and then when I look more closely there is nothing that looks less like Kate – it'll just be the way someone holds their head or walks. It's spooky. I swear I heard her laugh the other day . . .

I've got other friends, but I don't think I'll ever have a best friend like Kate, one who understood exactly what was going on in my head and what was going on at home, who I didn't have to explain things to, who just understood. The thing about Kate was, she didn't just look unusual, she *was* unusual, but she was more than that. I don't want to say precious or priceless like something in a museum, I mean, oh what's the word? Rare! That was it. Kate was rare.

Dujy and Armi

IRMA KURTZ – AUTHOR, TRAVEL WRITER AND
AGONY AUNT FOR *COSMOPOLITAN* AND *THE TIMES*

I had always wanted a sister. I yearned for a real soul
mate. I had a younger brother, but younger brothers
just aren't the same thing at all.

We were twelve when we met, Judy and I. We were
the closest that very best friends could be. We were so
close, as kids we had secret names for each other. She
was Dujy and I was Armi, and there was nothing we
wouldn't talk about, or do together. We lived in New
Jersey, twenty minutes from New York City, and by the
age of fourteen we were lying to our parents to escape
to the illicit excitement of Greenwich Village. We'd go
and hang out in coffee bars, sit about going to poetry
readings, listening to music and watching everything.
Of course we'd lie to our parents and pretend we were
having sleepovers at each other's houses; oh, you
know the tricks girls play.

I learned with Dujy that you could have a friendship without judgement, a friendship that was better
than having a sister. We shared everything – we even

had a crush on the same boy, but we never let it come between us. If anything, it drew us closer together, idolising him.

We loved gossiping. Swapping sex information was the greatest fun. Actually, it was sex *dis*-information, all hearsay about condoms and boys' equipment. At least I'd seen what a penis looked like (my younger brother's) but Dujy was an only child and hadn't got a clue. It was the 1950s in America and we all had an abiding fear of pregnancy – sex spelled pregnancy, and pregnancy meant shame.

What I guess we both had in common was that we both were born from troubled marriages. Neither of us knew what that trouble really was, but we comforted each other through the years of confusion. Later, I understood what we really shared was being a real disappointment to our mothers, who both wanted boys; it was like that in those days, having a girl first wasn't considered as good as having a boy. I even found the card my mother wrote to her mother, my grandmother, expressing such profound disappointment that I had turned out to be a girl. Parents would spend money on a son's education but not on a daughter's – it was thought to be a waste of money. Girls! What would they do with an education? So I went to the local high school with Dujy.

Dujy and I weren't exclusive best friends, clinging to each other in the playground, we were best friends amongst a load of friends, and we were popular. It was great. I trusted Dujy over and above anyone else, I told her my secrets, my fears, my longing to travel. She was the first person I shared my inner world with, I told her everything. She was the only teenage friend that I wasn't embarrassed to ask over when my parents were around – mostly because of my father's eating habits. To say he wasn't interested in table manners is putting it mildly – he shovelled food into his face – but he came from the ghetto, the Lower East Side.

Dujy and I shared so much together, but it was within those three to four years of changing from little girls and becoming women, that things changed. It was slow at first.

The first difficulties began when I was deemed to be bright and was streamed into other classes at school, a year higher. Dujy was immediately resentful, and began teasing me, calling me 'teacher's pet'. Things began to get a little funny between us, but we still always sat together at lunch and hung out after class.

Then one day even that changed. I went down to lunch and I can still remember what it felt like to be standing there in the cafeteria, holding my lunch tray, the carton of milk in front of me, the hamburger on my plate, my knife and fork. Dujy was sitting with another bunch of girls and for the first time ever, there was no space for me at the table. For the first time she hadn't saved a seat for me, and nobody bothered moving up. All the girls were behaving shiftily, and I can still see the look of cruel smugness on Dujy's face. I faltered for a moment not knowing whether to stay or go and then I realised, I knew, I was being frozen out. It only took a moment, that moment, and my whole world collapsed.

As I turned away I could hear them talking behind my back, and I knew they were talking about me. And after that, a whispering campaign began against me. I didn't know what I'd done wrong, other than win a national debating prize. I'd got sent to Chicago for the finals and when I returned, Dujy, my dear friend, had changed back into Judy. She was part of a different clique now and they weren't shy at showing their derogatory attitude towards me, and achievement. "Hey smart-ass!" they'd say, or "She thinks she's so smart," or "Why does she think she's so important and clever?" I was being told it was a bad thing to be clever, by people I thought were my friends.

It was bad enough losing Dujy as a friend, but quite another to gain her as an enemy. I cried all the way home that day and thought, "What's wrong with me, what have I done?"

When you have a best friend, you really have an ally against the world, a wall of defence. I thought I was going to be friends with Dujy for ever and then I was pushed out and I had no one else to go to and tell.

I was really hurt. The anger I felt I turned into pain and swallowed it whole. I had every reason to be angry at Dujy but she surrounded herself with a gang, and so there was never a showdown. That day in the cafeteria I just skulked away and from then on I worked even harder to get a scholarship and leave the small-mindedness of that world behind. I felt cheated; I had a real sense of heartbreak; in many ways it was more painful than splitting up from a lover . Men you can get over; a best friend is irreplaceable.

I still smile when I see best friends together. You can always recognise them from the way they laugh together. There's a certain joyous laughter that confidantes share, where things only have to be alluded to, and you know the other will understand, and together everything makes you laugh. It is the most joyous sound in the world. I think it's sometimes hard for men to understand the non-sex content, and the intensity of women's relationships.

Now I understand Dujy and I had grown apart. I was so voracious for knowledge and the world, I may have begun to look like trouble to Judy. I had started to go faster and maybe I had got a bit ahead of myself, had become a little scary with my obsessive reading. I was never going to be like my mother, or fulfill my parents' expectations, instead I was determined to escape to the world I read about in books. Whilst Judy was happy to fulfill her parents' expectations – you know how it was then: you had to marry a doctor or a lawyer, have children and be a housewife. It's what women were expected to do in the 1950s in America and Britain.

We didn't share the same dreams or expectations of life, Judy and I. It's hard when you start to drift apart because you want your friends to want what you want, to be part of your future fantasies and ambitions. My dreams were full of travelling and seeing the world, and living in Paris, but hers weren't. Maybe she realised my plans couldn't include her. We broke off so badly, at fifteen we were real enemies.

Eventually I got my scholarship and left home, and I travelled. I don't know what became of Judy, but I think in the end she would have stayed home and lived the life that was expected of her. It seemed like we were so similar but we were very different in the end. I learned something valuable from that particular experience: I have so many friends now that I know it's unfair to expect everything from one person. As an American in London, I've made a large family of my friends, and now I have London, I have an entire city as my best friend – and you can't beat that.

Aɴᴏᴛʜᴇʀ Lɪɴᴋ ɪɴ ᴛʜᴇ Cʜᴀɪɴ

A Cʜᴇʟᴛᴇɴʜᴀᴍ Lɪᴛᴇʀᴀʀʏ Fᴇsᴛɪᴠᴀʟ
COMPETITION WINNER
Flic, 13

Friendship to me is like a circle of chain links. If just one link is broken the whole thing falls apart and it becomes something entirely different. Each link is made from a different key role in being a best friend. Trust, loyalty, fun and knowledge of the other person are just a few of the links on the chain.

In all my thirteen years of living in this bustling, busy and boisterous world, I have had a lot of friendships – some great, others not so good.

A year ago, when I was just starting secondary school, I was extremely nervous. There were a few of us coming from my old school, but none that had been a really good friend. I knew that this was a time to start afresh and erase completely all the bullying and bad experiences of my past life.

Within my first week I was relieved to find that I made many new and good friends, and one of these was Anna. I first met Anna through another friend, who passed messages on to me through her. We needed this special way of communicating at first as we weren't in the same form, but soon we were spending all our lunch and break times together.

The year rapidly disappeared behind us in a blur of trips to town, phone calls every night and joyful meetings every day at school. It was as though any time spent apart was time wasted, and every experience only half as fun without Anna being there. My other friendships got put to one side; they didn't seem as important as the one I had with Anna, and so I discarded them in the way you do a warm coat when summer creeps up upon you. The end of the year came quickly and a school trip to France lay excitingly ahead of us. We choose our groups and who we'd be sharing dorms with so that we'd be with each other, and we couldn't wait to go away together.

The first couple of days were great – visits to the seaside, tours around cider farms and shopping in small French markets with delicious local food. Then on the third day a rumour started to go around about one of the teachers calling people names. The rumours got progressively nastier, resulting in lots of people taking sides and falling out.

Eventually, I had enough of all the scheming, gossip and lies. I decided to try to get to the bottom of it and find out who had started the whole thing in the first place. Who could have been so malicious as to ruin what was until that point a really fun holiday? To my dismay and utter disbelief I found out that the person who started it all off was my best friend, Anna. When I asked her about it, she said she had wanted to get her own back against her least favourite teacher. She'd been holding a grudge, and it wasn't even for any particular reason; she just didn't like her.

All of our year was in confusion: half siding with Anna, believing the rumours to be true, the other half with me, believing Anna had made it all up. I couldn't believe that I would ever be on the opposing side to Anna – she was my best friend. But what do you do when your friend starts to lie like a professional card shark, and to cause hurt to others by doing so? I could see Anna was digging herself into a deep, sticky cave of lies and the more she told, the larger and darker the hole grew, the more trapped she became.

It was such a mess that I decided to help her. The only way out I could see was to go and tell the teacher who it was and then for Anna to apologise. So I went ahead, and I truly thought I was doing the right thing in helping her to wipe the slate clean by being honest. I told the teacher what I knew, but when I suggested to Anna that she apologise, she was absolutely furious with me. It now seems obvious that she would be, but at the time I was surprised by her outburst. Then she tried to turn the other kids against me with lies. Instead of it making everything better and resolving all the intrigue and suspicions, what I did just made everything so much worse.

Now I could no longer bear to look at Anna and neither of us could even stand to be in the same room as each other. I switched dorms with one of my other friends, to prolong the time before I had to face her and eventually, as I knew I must, speak to her again.

Other friends told me of the other lies that she had been spreading about other people, and lies about other parts of her life. I was suddenly terrified that all of our friendship had been one great big lie. I didn't know what, if anything, of what she had said to me was truthful. That night I lay awake for hours, thinking things over and over in my head and in the end all I could do was cry myself to sleep and when I woke, my happy, bright world lay cold, grey and splintered.

My other friends were there for me and comforted me, even though, up till then, I had abandoned them all in favour of Anna's exclusive relationship, a relationship with a girl I hadn't really even known. Thankfully for me they were all really forgiving and lovely and welcomed me with open arms, straight back into their friendship circle.

Anna and I have now made friends again, not best friends but we can sit at the same table in a group and get on. We go to the same parties, even do school projects together but what was once there has now disappeared. It's sad but one crucial link in the chain is missing, and that is trust. I can never fully trust her again. And without that trust, a best friendship can never really exist.

Being best friends with Anna taught me how much I value the truth. One lie can so easily lead to another and very quickly you can end up living in a fantasy, a made-up world of your own, where no one really knows you, and you don't know them. You can easily become isolated by not being yourself; you can't connect properly with anyone because you are pretending to be something you think is more attractive to people, when what others actually value is the real you. In doing so, the old you is discarded and left to die. You become a robot, looking just the way you always have; you live and breathe as a normal person would, but within your web of fantasy and lies you feel nothing, because the emotions are all gone, eaten away by deceit.

Never Swap Diaries!

Sophie Ellis-Bextor
Singer and Songwriter
www.sophieellisbextor.net

Sarah and I grew up together. I see her now about once a year; but she was my very best friend from the time we were nine, all the way through our teens. Now that I'm married, I have my son and we don't work in the same field – all of this life stuff divides you. But we do share our past even though we don't have that much in common any more. The past must be strong enough to keep us together because she's always in the back of my mind. Even if we haven't seen each other for ages; I'll even dream about her.

We met before we even went to infant school. I remember being left to play with another little girl while my mum talked to some other woman in the park. Were we in a sandpit or sitting on the grass? It's hard to remember sometimes. It seems like a real memory, but maybe my mum told me about it later on and it became my memory from her story.

So Sarah and I started at infants at the same time and went through junior school together too. We didn't actually become best friends straight away.

When I met her, I wasn't meeting my shadow or anything like that. She had a best friend called Kiralee who was at the social centre of our class. Their parents were very friendly and I think forced them together a lot. At some point Sarah stopped wanting to be on Kiralee's sidelines, and we drifted or gravitated towards each other.

The thing about us was that we were always very different from each other. I was tall with dark brown hair and blue eyes and she was petite and blonde. Sarah was always very talented and incredibly creative; and I was never quite sure what I was good at. Sarah is one of those friends who's quiet, dependable, supportive and always so complimentary. She's neither as gregarious, nor as noisy as me. I've always found it very easy to be surrounded by people and to socialise with them, whilst Sarah is less outgoing. We would argue because we are both strong characters but we liked each other enough to always be able to make it up again.

As kids we spent a lot of time making things together. Sarah can make anything – jewellery, ornaments, clothes – she always had a great eye for fashion and I always loved dressing up, still do. For two or three years we lived in each other's homes. If I wasn't at hers, she was at mine.

Our parents had both separated at roughly the same time – when we were about three. We had both stayed with our mothers but saw our dads regularly. Sarah had an older brother, and I was an only child at that time. I think it suited us both to have a best friend who was in the same situation, who understood what it's like when your parents split up.

We were so close that when one of our fathers took us away on holiday, they'd always take us both. One year we stayed at my grandparents' house in the south of France with my father and his new wife. There was a storm one night and the curtains were being blown around the room and it was scaring us so we decided to tie and pin heavy things to the curtains to stop them. In the morning my dad came in and said, "What have you done to the curtains?"

I told him, and he asked why we didn't just shut the windows. We both burst out laughing! Of course it was obvious but the thought hadn't occurred to either of us, so we must be just the same on some level.

It's difficult going on holiday with other people's parents when you're ten and you don't have a mother or father there to stick up for you. I remember my dad making a joke out of something that Sarah had said – the way that she had said it – and her getting really embarrassed and upset at being made the centre of attention. Of course, my father didn't mean to humiliate her, he's just quite witty and gregarious, but I could feel her excruciating embarrassment.

Sarah's father once took just the three of us on

holiday to Spain. Poor man – it must have been a nightmare; he didn't realise the tears, screams, then silences that girl best friends are capable of, because when Sarah and I rowed, it was full on.

During the holiday, Sarah's father kept saying how great she was at swimming, drawing – actually, at most things. Her talents just gleamed, and I felt I wasn't really very good at anything in comparison. I suppose I wanted someone to be there for me, saying I was great, too. Instead, when he was taking pictures of us around the pool table one day, he told a local boy to put his arm around me and I almost died of embarrassment! I was interested in boys, but I wasn't quite ready for the real thing. He didn't understand that. My resentment built up and I poured it into my diary.

One afternoon we were sitting around our hotel room, a little bored I guess, when Sarah and I thought it was a good idea to read each other's diaries. It wasn't. At that age you write exactly what you feel – totally from your perspective, very directly – and you don't consider other people. So when I read Sarah's diary and she had written about how she didn't like my father because he was cruel and when she read in my diary that I didn't like *her* father, all hell broke loose. You don't want your friends complaining about your parents. However much you might grumble about them to the rest of the world, only *you* are actually allowed to do it.

Sarah locked me out of the hotel room and I sat outside in the corridor trying to talk to her, trying to convince her to let me back in. I felt that if I was in the same room as her she could at least see my expression and me hers, even if she wouldn't speak to me. As it was I was so frustrated and angry I burst into tears. The screaming and crying on both sides of the door went on for what seemed like hours until we were both worn out. The worse thing was we knew we had to be with each other for another five days until we flew home; we had reached an impasse. Then one of us made a joke, and the other one laughed, and of course we made up.

That day taught me a great lesson. I realised that some people are more sensitive than others and that I must be careful not to trample over others' feelings.

Everything changed at the end of junior school. I remember that last day. All the girls hysterical with tears, as if they were all being sent away; when in fact they were all going on to the same big comprehensive nearby and it was only me that was being sent off elsewhere. I really wanted to go with Sarah, but my parents had decided to send me to a private school. We moved house at the same time, but Sarah and I made an effort to keep in touch and for the first couple of years managed it quite well, seeing each other at weekends. I didn't think I'd ever fit into my new school. I felt peculiar, like the odd one out, where all the girls seemed to wear capes and had their own horses, but slowly I found the other fish out of water, and I settled into a group of friends.

When we were around fifteen, on the weekends, we started to go out clubbing and I would always invite Sarah to come too. She was always very quiet and didn't really appear to be enjoying herself. Sometimes it seemed as if she didn't say an entire word through the whole night of us laughing and dancing. At that point I thought, 'We're growing apart; one day we'll just stop calling each other'.

By the time we were eighteen we really didn't have much in common any more and by twenty-one we were going in totally different directions. That was when she started to crop up in my dreams, and I did in hers, as if we were being prompted to call and tell each other about our dreams. And that's when we got back in touch again.

I suppose Sarah knows me in a different way to most of the people who are my friends now. I am a loyal girl, I don't make new friends very easily and I spend a lot of my time with my family. I don't like trapping myself in new things. Some people in my industry, the music world, think that if they surround themselves with the packaging of celebrity – the friends, the image, the lifestyle – they'll be less likely to lose it. For me, it's the opposite. I don't want to ever feel that losing any of that, would make any difference to me.

Now I feel Sarah and I will probably know each other for the rest of our lives. We do different things, we've never looked anything like each other, but it doesn't matter. I feel such incredible warmth towards her; we've been through so much together, a whole history of growing up.

In truth, it's usually always me who calls her ... oh my God! Maybe ... maybe she's hoping that one day I'll stop calling her! Now that's funny, I hadn't thought of that before.

I Saw Them

Amelia, 13

I first met my best friend in Pizza Hut. You never can tell where you're going to meet someone who will become really special – and later turns out to be your worst nightmare.

You know that saying, 'Friends over boys', or whatever it is? Yeah? Oh, you know, 'Boys may come and go, but best friends last for ever'. Well, I've just found out that it is complete and utter rubbish, especially when it comes to the stupid cow who, amazingly, used to be my best friend and has now stabbed me neatly in the back. And it's all over a boy called Luke who, I was certain, obviously preferred me to her, but she couldn't see that.

How could she do this to me? What is going on in her tiny little brain, when she knows I love him? And she's known I love him ever since that stupid heart-spilling day in my room when I told her everything.

God, I hate her! Eliza – for that is her evil name – really is the biggest bitch I've ever known on this planet. I know all that now and yet I still can't quite believe my eyes, though they've never been wrong before. I don't even wear glasses. She has trapped him with her sly ways, like a spider who has woven the most complicated and deceptively alluring lace web, and he is the tiny fly. Oh Eliza, Eliza, is definitely the spider. Don't get me wrong, if Luke was a fly he'd be the most gorgy fly ever. Of course, Luke isn't anything like a fly . . . oh, just forget the analogy thing.

Though it pains me to say it, because I have to relive the scene again in my mind's eye, I saw them – I SAW THEM. Eliza and Luke. They were just down the hill from my house, merged together, snogging, and so close they'd almost become one. I might never get the image out of my head. I was shocked, I couldn't believe it – it was so horrible. I just stood there for about fifteen seconds, looking, seeing but not wanting to see or believe what was in front of me, my mouth gaping open like a fish at feed. Fifteen seconds – though it felt like fifteen centuries. I had to face the facts. My up-till-then-very-best-friend had betrayed me. I gave her one huge glare, whether she saw or not I didn't care, but I knew she felt it, my paralysing glare. I prayed that looks could kill (if only) and then ran. Ran, ran away and home as fast as I could to lock myself in my room.

I'm stuck in my room. I can't go downstairs because Mum will know I've been crying, she senses it and she'll be so sympathetic, and I can't stand the sympathy because it just makes for so much more crying. Oh, I hate tears! Practically since I've been born, all I seem to do is cry and I hate crying, as much as I now hate Eliza. I blame my dad for dying, and making Mum cry all the time. No, I know that's not fair. It wasn't his fault, he didn't want to die and it's not Mum's fault that he's dead, however much she apologises. It was so many years ago now. I can't think about it any longer.

The problem is, I'm stuck in my room until I don't look like I've been crying, which means I'm never coming out. I might as well throw away the key. I try to distract myself with a funny book. Sometimes it can make you stop thinking about the mess that life is steeped in. Sometimes it can help. I chose *Knocked Out by My Nunga-Nungas* by Louise Rennison, who usually makes me laugh, but her heroine, Georgia, has boy problems of her own, and it keeps leading my mind back to Eliza the Slut, Queen Bitch of the Universe. I can't help it – every cell in my body is yelling it. The tears might have stopped a little but I am so angry that the only way to channel my fury is to beat up my pillow. I beat it until it is as battered as cod and chips, as battered as an old, rusty, beat-up car, and then I have to try to sleep on it. On the other hand, does it matter, since I'm never going to sleep ever again?

* * *

Monday arrives alarmingly quickly and I know I have to face Eliza at school. That's so ... *great* – NOT. I'm dreading it. What to say to a betraying, evil ex-best friend? There aren't the words in my vocabulary. There are no words that have ever been invented to describe how I feel about this nightmare experience. How do I say what I feel? *Can* I say how I feel? If only I was a politician, then somebody could write my script for me.

Thank goodness for assembly. Did I think I'd ever say that? Luckily I am able to escape her right at the beginning of the school day, because for the whole of the morning we have to sit alphabetically and her name begins with Y and mine with E. Up until now, before all of this stuff with Luke happened, Monday morning was my least favourite school day because I didn't get to sit next to Eliza; now it's a BIG plus.

Eventually, at break time, Eliza tracks me down. She catches up with me and waves in my face like nothing's happened, as if everything is normal between us. On what planet is she living? She's going to get one hell of a shock – I hope the shock is so large she gets sent to casualty. I move towards her little waving hand and stand in front of her, glaring at her. I see her lips move – I think she is asking me what's wrong, but I can barely hear her. I am trying to think about what to do, but the blood is pumping so hard in my head, it fills my ears. A voice in my head says, 'If she smiles at you with all that pretend innocence, you're going to have to slap her – no, *punch* her, to the ground.'

It only takes a faint trace of a smile to encourage me. I draw my fist back and feel my body position itself in a karate stance. (It's automatic – I am a blue belt.) I whack her hard in the face and she falls to the floor. "BITCH!" I shout down at her. She struggles to stand up, her nose dripping blood down to her lip and I don't care. I just don't care. I stare back at her in disgust, and I can't even register how she looks at me.

Suddenly I notice the complete quiet on the concourse, and a pain in my clenched fist. Nobody ever tells you how much it hurts to hit someone. Then everyone starts goading us on – "Catfight, catfight, catfight . . ." Their voices grow stronger and louder into a chant, until the teacher on duty appears. She helps Eliza off the floor and sends her to see the nurse, and then takes me off to the dreaded room E3A. This is where only the people in really serious trouble get taken. I'd only ever been there once before, when I was being bullied in Year Seven. I never thought I'd be going back for being the bully.

It is a plain white room with nothing in it but a table and a chair. There is nothing to look at, not even a window to gaze out of. It's basically like prison, solitary confinement for the whole day, but you can't even go to sleep, because the teachers send work in for you to do. You just have to become a robot. I think the idea is to think about what you've done. The day passes very slowly and eventually they let me out after an extra half-hour of detention, and it's time to go home.

I get inside the door of our house and Mum says there's a message for me on the answerphone.

"'Katie, it's Eliza. Have you heard? Luke's going to live in Australia. He's leaving next week with his family. I'm so sorry I fancied him too. Really, I am so sorry, I don't know what to say. But I guess both of our hearts are broken now so . . . I just wondered what you were up to . . . I mean, do you want to grab a pizza in town? I could meet you at Pizza Hut. Ring me back as soon as you get this message. Please.'"

I slump against the hall wall as I listen to the message. I can't help the half-smile that plays across my lips. We'd met at Pizza Hut at the beginning, before all of this nightmare. Maybe with Luke away in Australia, just maybe, we can make up . . . I don't even bother taking off my coat before I call out to Mum, "Mum, I'm going out . . ."

Two of the Rockettes

Cathy Hopkins – author
www.cathyhopkins.com

I met Annie when I changed convent schools in
Manchester in Year Nine. I was dreading the start of
the new September term as I knew that all the friendships would already have been established from Year
Seven. I remember my first day well, with everyone
greeting their friends after the holiday. I felt so alone.
The new girl. I couldn't see where I was going to fit, or
how I was going to make friends. And then I saw
Annie. She was in front of me in the line at the school
assembly, her dark hair cut into a Vidal Sassoon short
bob which curved into three perfect Vs in the nape of
her neck. I was well impressed. Here was a girl who
clearly knew a thing or two about style, something I
needed badly, coming from a family with five brothers, no sisters and a mother whose idea of a haircut
was to put a pan on my head and clip round it until
my hair looked pudding-shaped. (She swears that she
never did this and took great care with my haircuts,
but I had to live with the results and I say: pan, pud-
ding.)

Annie and I started hanging out together soon after I'd set my sights on her, and although our home lives were different (she had two elder sisters), we discovered that we had a lot in common and a similar sense of humour. We seemed to spend a lot of our time laughing. We only needed a bag of dolly mixtures on the way home on the bus, after spending the day trying on clothes in town, and we were happy. Some days my jaw would ache from having laughed so much. It was a wonderful age of discovery: music (soul, Tamla Motown), fashion (Chelsea Girl, Biba, Miss Selfridge), books, make-up, boys, and a best friend to do it all with. Plus, she owned a calf-length tan suede coat which was top of most teens' want-list back then. I hoped that some of her cool would rub off on me as I trooped along beside her in some mismatched outfit, usually cobbled together from cast-offs.

On Friday nights we went to St Bernadette's youth club on Princess Parkway, (Judy Finnegan from *Richard and Judy* used to go there too, apparently) where we would dance the night away, and then go and snog one of the boys we had crushes on in the car park afterwards. It was difficult for me sometimes as I had shot up tall, five-foot-nine at fifteen, and most of the boys only came up to my chest (not that they objected, eye to chest was OK by most of them). Having to stoop over to snog never felt totally romantic to me, though. Neither did the car park. Annie was lucky in that she was the same height as the boys. Even more luckily, we never fancied the same boys, so we never fell out over any of them.

There seemed to be two types of girls back then, ones like Annie and me, who liked to hang out in a big group and not get too serious; and ones who started dating at fourteen and stayed with the same boy for two years at a time. I preferred the company of my mates. More laughs, less hassle and they didn't try to grope you.

At sixteen we pretended to be eighteen and went to clubs in town and then we started hanging out at the uni bar at Manchester University with the students. We'd usually go back to someone's place and listen to music and snog boys to the sounds of Crosby, Stills and Nash, the Grateful Dead or Neil Young. I remember a guy called Tony Jelly waxing lyrical about burning your bra (for Women's Lib) and then stealing mine. When I got home, I ran upstairs fast, petrified that my mum could tell I wasn't wearing one.

After our O-levels, I stayed on to do my A-levels while Annie went to work in a bank, but it wasn't for her. She was too creative for that kind of job, so she went to college in Bath to study dance. I went on to Art College. At some point she came back and rented a room in our house in Manchester. That was a great era. My parents had gone away to work in Zimbabwe (then Rhodesia) and left me and my eldest brother

Stephen in charge of our family home. We rented out rooms to our friends and, for a time, life seemed like one long party, although I must have attended some lectures and classes, not that I can remember much of them. Most of the avant-garde of Manchester lived or passed through the house at some time or other during that period, including legendary poet John Cooper Clarke who vowed to write a poem about Annie because of her name, Anne O'Malley – an anomaly. Hope he does some day.

At that time Annie and I were in a band called Driving Rock and the Rockettes. We were two of the Rockettes (there were three). It was doo-wap rock and roll, and we used to tour universities as the warm-up act before bigger, more famous bands. So much for the glamour of being a chick singer though – my main memories are of the surreal world of motorway services at two a.m. in the morning. I left eventually, because I'd had enough of sitting in the back of a transit van on the M6, jammed in with the other musicians, roadies, assorted girlfriends and sound equipment on the way back from gigs. I wanted to be Joni Mitchell or Grace Slick. Annie wanted to be Joni or Carole King. To relieve the boredom of the long journeys, we'd sit in the back and wail along into the night together.

Annie is still my best friend all these years later. Yes, there were times in our twenties and thirties when our lives went in different directions and we didn't see each other as much but we always kept in touch with cards, letters and phone calls. And now whenever I go back to Manchester to visit my family, I always see Annie, and she regularly visits me in London. Nothing has changed between us, even if we haven't seen each other for ages; within five minutes we're back where we were, fourteen again.

I can't think we've ever fallen out. No, I'm sure we haven't. I mean, there might have been times when we didn't like the people the other was hanging out with, but those people have come and gone. We've stayed the distance. The only time I do remember feeling miffed with her was back in Year Nine when at lunch times at school we'd act out being Diana Ross and the Supremes. I never got to be Diana. I always got relegated to being a Supreme. Pff. Must have that out with her one of these days! Apart from that, ours has been an equal friendship. For her fiftieth, we decided it would be a blast to get the old band Driving Rock and the Rockettes back together. It was brilliant. We'd all changed a little, thirty years on (balder, fatter, more wrinkled – and that's just me) but it felt like that movie, *The Commitments*.

I guess Annie's the sister I've never had – in fact, she's like another member of my family. We all love her. She hasn't got an ounce of malice or bitchiness in her body and I know I could tell her anything. And she's a true optimist. She bounces back from whatever life hurls at her and sees a way forward. We still make each other laugh. It's a great feeling to know that she's there. Apart from my family, there is no one else that I've stayed in touch with since my formative years in such a close way. I know that I am very lucky to have a friendship that has lasted so long.

Cow

LANA, 19

You think as you get older that you'll get over being scared of stuff, like the first day in a new place. I still remember how scared I was going into nursery class for the first day, and then junior school, and definitely secondary school. That felt like a jungle full of wild animals, but finally I got used to it – I figured maybe I'd become one of the wild animals.

Anyway, the first day of university was just the same – new girl, knowing no one, and not only at a new campus but I'd moved to the city too, and it was all bigger, stranger, more difficult. It was like being in a foreign country where you can work the currency, even speak the language, but you don't quite understand what's going on.

I was living on my own in a bedsit. Sometimes I was so lonely at night in those first weeks I'd bite the pillow trying not to cry. I wanted to go home so badly that I couldn't even tell my parents. If I started to cry on the phone, I'd pretend I was really busy and that I had to get off the phone, or a friend had appeared.

Anything not to show how bad it all was.

The greyness of the skies in the first month seemed to commiserate – they'd open their heavens and bleed tears over me on the way home. Then I remembered something my mum had always taught me to do: smile (she's a very positive type of person, the sort whose cup is always half full, who would make us do a jiggety hoppy dance if ever my brother and I started to cry when we were young). She said it might feel odd, smiling when you're sad or unhappy, but it changes you.

"It's a bit like putting the kettle on: it has to boil before you get the joy of that first cup of tea." And so I smiled. Felt nothing, but kept on smiling – and that was how I got my nickname at college, Smiley.

I thought our tutor was being ironic when he first called me Smiley, making fun of me – but then everyone else started to call me that too. I suppose it made me a bit of a talking point, along with the fact that I did paintings of angels. Not the saccharin, cherubic type, they were more like people than chocolate box covers or valentine cards.

One day I was painting in the studio. It was still the first term and this bunch of girls came in. They looked so much older than the rest of us and they had to be from the degree department. They were nosing around, looking at everyone else's work, and then they came over to me.

One of them said, "Hey, you must be Smiley, I've heard about you. Is this one of your Angel paintings?" I think that was Rosy.

"God, they are really weird," said Gail.

"But in a good way," said India and smiled at me. "I like them. You'll have to come and see our studio."

And that was how I became friends with India. It seemed so simple. Every day I saw her and the others at college, and we hung out at lunch or went to the pub after college. Sometimes we would just hang around their studio, drinking coffee. Suddenly I had new friends, friends who rang me up and took me to parties. India and I both had a passion for markets and we'd get up at ridiculous times to go scavenging through them for vintage clothes or old records and stuff. We would go to any foreign film playing – you try finding someone with a mutual love of films with subtitles.

The only thing I suppose that sometimes marred our friendship was her boyfriend, Simon. The first time I met him I didn't like him – too fond of his own voice, always had to be right, one of those sorts. He knew he was handsome, and I hate vanity. Confident and handsome. I suppose it made me feel inferior because I was also younger than them. They weren't getting on too well and you could see it was more of a habit relationship than a burning passion. They were always slagging each other off behind the other's back, and sometimes in front of people. Well, you don't do that when you're in love with someone. Not if you really love them, even when they're fantastically irritating. I'd ask India why she was still with Simon if she felt that way, but she'd always say, "You don't understand, Lana. We're going to get married. We've made all the plans, which means we can say these things and it doesn't make any difference."

She was right, I didn't understand.

Then they had three big fights, one after another in one week, and the final one involved her smashing a plate over his head; throwing a bottle of perfume at him that smashed, stinking the place out; and saying she never wanted to see him again. I know because I was at the party when it happened and had to duck. I'd like to say it was a real love-hate relationship, but it seemed there was never any love, just plenty of hate. Now that I think about it, a lot of the time India and I were together was spent discussing the flaws in Simon's character. The conversation was the same one over and over again – I would play devil's advocate, always putting his side of the argument forward. And then, gradually, despite my initial dislike for him and his handsome confidence, I began to see how unreasonable India was being about Simon. She was terribly judgemental.

I began to notice that India was the sort of girl who'd laugh at other girls in the corridor, because their skirt wasn't the right shape, length or colour for the season. It made me feel uncomfortable that she wanted to make herself feel better by making others look like fools, but I thought well, that's what happens if you tie yourself to your boyfriend, even if you hate them. It makes you miserable.

India went away to visit her parents and to get over Simon after their row just as the holidays came, but I had a job by then, working in a restaurant, so I wasn't going anywhere over the four weeks of Easter. One day, on my way to work, I saw Simon coming towards me.

"Hey, Smiley! What's up?" He asked with this big grin. I was surprised by his friendliness.

"Oh, I'm OK. Just off to work, evening shift."

"What time do you finish?"

"Around midnight, why?"

"Great! There's a boom party tonight, doesn't start till twelve. I could pick you up if you like."

I found myself saying OK, because I assumed that the gang must be going. I mean, I didn't think anything was strange, except for the weird way he was looking at me.

I noticed he had a picnic basket when he collected me. It was a really warm evening, more like summer than Easter, and we walked towards the park and down to the lake with all the silly duck and geese lit up by the pink park lights. He stopped, opened the basket and got out a rug, a bottle of champagne, two glasses and a box of smoked salmon sandwiches and asked me to sit down. You can imagine how confused I was. "But Simon, where's the party?" I asked.

"It's here of course. Do you like champagne?"

I said something witty like, "Only to bathe in." Then suddenly he started kissing me. I didn't expect it. I thought I had never flirted with him, but maybe I did. I knew what I was doing was wrong, but I couldn't help myself; I couldn't stop myself from kissing him back. And then we sat there drinking and talking until the sky began to lighten and the sun rose. And it was so lovely, I mean just everything about it was perfect, maybe because it was such a surprise. That kiss changed everything. I looked at Simon that night, and it was as if I saw him for what he was for the first time – gorgeous, sympathetic, sexy, sweet and warm. He talked about India and all the problems they'd had together for so long, and why it was such a relief to break up. I did feel disloyal talking about her behind her back, but he was there and she wasn't.

India got back a week later, rang me up going absolutely mental. I'd been seeing Simon practically every night, and I wasn't thinking about India. I wasn't thinking about anything – I was soaked in the impracticalities and mind-washing loveliness of *lurve*. I was too busy to think about the reality of life – I even left my portfolio on the bus.

"How could you do it!" she screamed down the phone. "You knew I was going to marry him. I told you. You . . . COW!"

Angry people always seem so funny, I almost mooed back, it seemed so ridiculous, especially when I was floating in a state of loved-up bliss. "But you weren't going out any more," I countered.

"We had one little row, we were getting back together and he was coming to stay with my parents and me this weekend."

"But he told me you were finished."

"And who are you going to believe – your best friend, or some lying toe-rag, huh?" And suddenly she reminded me about our friendship. I felt evil.

"I don't know. I'm sorry India. I never wanted to hurt you."

"What, cow? Nice way of repaying my kindness. Don't expect to have any friends next term. Oh and another thing. Never try to speak to me again. I don't talk to common prostitutes."

India never spoke to me again, but I heard her laugh at my clothes plenty of times in the corridor with Rosy. I didn't expect her to forgive me but I never thought it would be such 'pout-right' war for the rest of the year. Talk about lipsticks at dawn! Let's just say I stopped being called Smiley and it was tough, but I had Simon.

Unfortunately Simon and I split up when I changed

college, because I moved down south. I've thought about it a lot since, asked myself, was it worth stealing my best friend's boyfriend? I don't know whether I was stupid, or just desperate to have some affection. I still don't feel I was entirely wrong. I didn't steal him, but maybe I'm fooling myself because I don't want to feel guilty? Whatever, I don't know, maybe I was just so lonely I wanted someone to fill that emptiness. How sad am I? Boo hoo hoo.

Or, maybe India was right . . . maybe I *am* a right cow? But I don't think so, and at least I don't laugh at what people wear.

SPECIAL

VANESSA FENTON – ROYAL BALLET DANCER
AND CHOREOGRAPHER

It was a beautiful, beautiful friendship. Too special, I'd say. When you get that close to someone, in a way you know you won't be able to maintain it forever. Like the intensity of the colour and smell of a flower when it blooms.

We were eleven when we first met, at the Royal Ballet boarding school in Richmond. Every year about five thousand kids audition for one of twenty-eight places. The year we started we all knew without a doubt what an enormous privilege it was to be there, and that we were expected to be extremely disciplined, to work hard, very hard – and we did. There was nothing we wouldn't do in order to achieve our aim of being the best; to be perfect. He was the closest person to me in the most desperate and trying of times. For four teenage years, he really was the only person I could talk to. Why? It wasn't because I didn't like the other girls, it was because he was so different from all the others.

He was beautiful, really beautiful, but the respect I

had for him was for his incredible passion – intellectual and creative. He dared to be different when we were all being taught to conform. We weren't friends straight away, but once we were, once we discovered we were soul mates, we were inseparable – bonded together against the world.

Neither of us came from families that were involved in dancing or the ballet world. I come from the country and my family didn't want me to go away, but at ten and a half I was determined to be a ballet dancer. I wanted to make my family proud, to show them that I could do it. Not just another little girl who wanted to be a pretty ballerina, but a proper, respected dancer. It was hard at first. I'd never been away from home for such long periods and I saw my parents only once every three weekends during the school year and spoke to them on the phone for five minutes every three days. All that emotion has to go somewhere – of course it goes into your dancing – but it's inevitable that you form close relationships in that fiercely competitive environment.

I was friends with the girls at ballet school, but the friendship I had with him was completely different, so much more intense. Then and now I take my friendships very seriously – you have to, to be able to trust friends with all your confidences. I was his only friend and that meant a lot to me. In the end I'd far rather have one really good friend than four who are half-hearted.

We were the very best of friends from twelve through to sixteen. During those four years I watched as he tried to be the best ballet dancer possible, and as the world of ballet slowly tried to destroy his originality, stamping him down. It's a very tough world, the ballet world. You can't show any emotion except when you are dancing. As a ballet dancer you have to be able to take criticism and not react; you learn not to cry and you learn to swallow all the pain and all the anger. Sometimes I would say to him when he was hurt and upset at some criticism, "Shout at me, I can take it!" but he didn't and that only seemed to make things worse. I would watch as he climbed slowly, silently, back inside himself.

He was ninety-three per cent perfect as a ballet dancer when only ninety-eight to one hundred per cent is allowable (the two per cent leverage is because we are, after all, humans and not automatic robots) – and ninety-three per cent just isn't to enough perfection in the ballet world. There isn't the space for mistakes or to not be perfect. In his eyes he'd failed by not being the best. The best dancers of the year were always the most popular, everybody in the school always loved them the most and the boys always liked the girls who could do the most pliés (a ballet movement where the knees are bent and the back is kept straight).

It wasn't that he was never good enough, it was

simply that the body he was born with wasn't perfect for ballet dancing. It doesn't matter how good you are, or how creative as a ballet dancer – if your pelvis doesn't turn in the right way, or you grow too tall, or your body isn't in proportion, you won't succeed.

In a ballet school, some boys struggle with their sexuality and try to be very male, very heterosexual. He didn't, but because he wasn't the very best dancer and because he wasn't ultra heterosexual, the other boys always used to pick on him. I tried to defend him, as his only friend, but I wasn't always successful.

It's hard to explain how brave he was at speaking out, how he dared to be so different in every way possible in such a conservative environment. He was an original, and he wasn't going to conform just to be part of it. He was so talented – writing, dancing, composing music and choreographing whole ballets at fourteen – that he really inspired people.

Ballet has to be your whole life while you're training. It's difficult to compare ballet school to a normal school, or ballet training to what other teenagers do. On top of your normal academic subjects you spend the rest of your time learning everything about ballet, not just how to dance, but how to memorise your steps and the nuances of music, the discipline. Exercise classes and rehearsals fill your day and night. You have to be totally driven, obsessive about your diet and shape as well as dancing and music. Every day we did all that together – day in, day out. Now, as an adult, I am able to remember every movement and the music of dozens of ballets in my head.

We both got into the upper school at sixteen, only eight girls and eight boys are chosen – the others fall by the wayside. He didn't want to stay on, so he left to go and study somewhere else. We've stayed in touch – time and distance didn't and won't affect our friendship ever, I'm certain. We've been through so much together and that binds you. As I said, we were soul mates and that never changes. I haven't seen him for about a year but I know he's doing well. If I bumped into him in the street right now our relationship, love, respect and friendship would still be the same; nothing would have changed.

To this day, I've never met anyone who is as brave, who fought to be himself with such courage and conviction, and to be that brave is an amazing thing – but then, he'll always be an amazing person.

Baby Sister

Carmen, 14

Ella, my sister, was always my best friend. It didn't matter that she was older than me and teased me sometimes because she looked after me too. Ever since I can remember I'd really loved being with her, we got on. We were always laughing together, not like some other brothers or sisters.

At school we both had friends in our own classes, our own age, and most of the time when we were there, break times and stuff, we ignored each other. But back at home it was different. We would play together for hours. Monopoly was our favourite, then cards – Snap or Black Jack – and all sorts of games where we would invent our own special rules.

In the summer we would sit out on our garden bench, reading comics or stories to each other, plaiting each other's long hair in more and more complicated styles. A tube of Smarties would last us hours because we'd lick the coloured shells and paint our faces with them, red on our cheeks, yellow on our eyes, and pink on our lips, as if it was make-up, and then we'd eat the chocolate up. We'd make houses for our cats out of cardboard boxes and whatever else we could find in the dusty old shed at the side of the house. The shed was great because it was full of rusty tricycles, broken lawnmowers, gardening and DIY stuff, and nobody ever went in it except for spiders and us. We spent whole afternoons making rabbit runs and mini adventure playgrounds, but the cats, Posh and Max, were never interested until Ella put chocolate drops or cheese in a trail to encourage them in. She was always having ideas and we were never bored because Ella would always say, "I know let's . . ." and we would.

Mum has to work and she's never there when we get home from school and sometimes she has to work on weekends too, so we have to find things to do. Often we'd go swimming or to the library when it was raining, and to the park if it was sunny. We liked to read all the same books – detective stories and mysteries.

I am younger than Ella, but only by a year; people were always mistaking us for twins. Pretending we were twins seemed more interesting than just being plain sisters, plus we both had brown hair and blue eyes, though Ella is a bit bigger than me. We used to say, "Of course, we're not identical," and then burst out laughing; it was our joke. There were lots of things that were different about us, but not so much that people wouldn't believe we were twins – we even talked the same. What made us even closer was our circumstances, both of us at home alone without Mum or any grown-ups.

When we were younger we couldn't invite friends home because they might tell their parents that we had no adults looking after us and it might get Mum into trouble. It isn't Mum's fault that she has to work so much; since Dad left it's hard for her and I know she'd rather be with us, but she can't. Besides, sometimes we preferred being on our own, with no adult to boss us around. We were fine, just Ella and me. Nothing bad ever happened to us. The worst that happened was when Ella dared me to drink some of Mum's perfume and I did and I was sick. Yuck!

Mum's always home by seven and then we have dinner and talk about what's happened, have baths, watch telly, go to bed; usual stuff. Tucked up in our bunk beds, we would talk each other to sleep with imagined stories of our lives as grown-ups, all our dreams and nightmares. We would take it in turns. Sometimes I didn't want my turn and I would ask Ella to tell me more about her dreams – she always seemed to have more of a story than I did. She could talk for ever about when she was going to be a famous movie star.

Ella's going to live in America, have a house with a swimming pool in the Hollywood hills where all the best film stars live, and another by the beach in

Malibu. She's going to be as beautiful as Halle Berry, win an Oscar and wear designer gowns to premieres and walk along red carpets having her picture taken. She'll have a wardrobe so big there will be five hundred dresses, just for the evening, and each will have a matching pair of shoes and handbag. Each morning she will have her hair and nails done. She's even going to have her own private mini cinema to watch movies in, with a special machine to make popcorn and a fridge filled with lemonade.

I could tell when she was coming to the end of her dream story because she'd always add, "Of course, I won't be there much because I will have to travel all over the world . . ."

And that was when I would add, "But I'll never see you, Ella."

And she would reply, "Of course you will. You will be my Personal Assistant. You'll go everywhere with me and organise everything."

"OK," I'd say and go to sleep, happy that I was part of the dream, Ella's future.

Then everything changed. The trouble started last year, when I didn't say my usual, "OK". It was the afternoon, we'd just got in from school, and Ella told me once more about her Hollywood dream. But this time, when she said that I'd be her Personal Assistant, I said, "But, Ella, I'm going to be too busy running my farm.

I won't be able to just get up and leave the animals, they can't feed themselves."

I've always wanted to live on a farm in the middle of the countryside with lots of animals. This is *my* dream: I'll feed the chickens every day and eat their eggs, ride my horse, Blue (that's what I'm going to call him), eat real apples that I pick off my own apple trees. I will have cats and dogs, pigs and turkeys and you can't just leave all those animals every time your sister wants you to travel as her assistant. Animals can't look after themselves.

When I said no, she got so angry she started screaming and shouting. "Well, don't be my PA. I'm offering you the chance to meet famous people and have a wonderful life, but you'd rather feed pigs. I don't care, I wouldn't want you anyway – you'd probably be bog useless!"

Then I started crying because, well, I didn't think I'd be useless and I didn't like Ella thinking that I would be useless. She told me to stop being such a baby, and unless I did straight away she wouldn't be friends with me again. I said I didn't want to be her friend if she kept on shouting at me and she looked at me as if she really hated me – as if *I* was the bitch – and then she slapped me round the face. I ran off to the loo and locked myself in and cried and cried until I'd run out of tears. My face was so hot I had to put a cold flannel on it to stop it being red. When I came out she'd gone. I sat with Max on my lap for hours before she came home; I stroked him until I felt better. When she came back, we didn't mention the slap – we've never mentioned it. We pretended to make up, I suppose, but it's never been the same; things aren't the way they used to be.

We don't spend much time doing anything together now. We never pretend to be twins any more, Ella has her hair in an Afro while mine's still plaited. Anyway we're older now and it would be silly – nobody would believe we're twins.

I remember the next day after our row. Ella didn't find me after school. She texted me on my mobile telling me to go home by myself – she was going over to Chelsea's for tea. I didn't go home, I went to the library to do my homework. That's what I do every day after school now with my friend Sal, and when we finish we play on the computer, or make up dances to our favourite songs as we walk back from the library singing. We like watching DVDs and drawing. Sal's so funny – she's always making jokes.

Mum asked us the other day, "What's happened to you two? Ella, why aren't you ever with Carmen no more? You girls used to spend all your time together, now I never see you in the same room. You stay with Carmen this afternoon while I work."

And Ella said, "Mum, I can't. I promised Chels and Iz. Besides I'm not hanging with Carm – she's too much of a baby. Boohoo this, wah wah that, honestly!"

I know she's my sister and everything but sometimes, actually most of the time, I really, really hate her, she's such a bitch! She might be my sister but there is nothing that she could do or say that would ever in the history of the world, ever, ever convince me to have her as a friend again, and I don't care how famous she gets, or who knows it, and that's the plain, honest, truth!

All About the Effort

Beatrice, 17

My parents were always taking me on holiday when I was young. Twice a year we'd go and stay at some ritzy hotel on sandy white and golden beaches in different parts of the world. For a week or two, we'd lie around the pool and do nothing, but I always longed to meet a friend of my own age. I'm sure it was nice for Mum and Dad, lying about reading and sunbathing, but it would have been nicer for me if there had been kids my age there. More often than not I would be the only child playing in the pool, diving for coins for myself. Luckily, since I was used to being an only child, I had invented a fleet of imaginary friends, so I always had them about to play with, but I liked real ones better.

If a child appeared I immediately made friends with them, and my mother would 'adopt' them for as long as we were staying there. My parents were always very welcoming and would treat my new friends as if they'd always been part of our family. On the odd occasion that I became friends with a girl the same age as me and her parents wanted to take me on outings with their daughter, my mother always said no. She didn't like letting me out of her sight, she was kind of overprotective. I suppose that was because I was an only child.

I'd never tell these holiday two-week best friends all my real deep secrets, because I suppose I always knew that they were short-term flings. However much we promised to keep in contact and be forever the bestest of friends, like the turquoise-tiled pool, the endless blue sky, sunshine and soft sand beaches – it wasn't going to last. Maybe out of context, these two-week friendships wouldn't work. Maybe it's too damp and cold for them to last back home in Britain. I don't know.

I'd tell my imaginary friends all my deepest secrets, my *secret* secrets, and that was all I needed. Imaginary friends are great – they are always supportive, as crazy and as fun as you want them to be. There is nothing that an imaginary friend won't do for you – they'll always play the games that you choose and never fight over who won. They'll do anything for you – other than become real. That's the problem.

When I was growing up, my mum loved me to wear dresses. There's nothing wrong with dresses, except that these were always really girly ones, like little dollies' dresses. In fact, she would often get matching dresses for me and my dolls, which, now I think about it, is a little weird. Me and my doll would go everywhere together wearing the same outfits! But I can't blame my mum, really. My grandma was obsessed with dolls too. She loved those really old porcelain dolls in costumes from foreign countries.

It wasn't until I got to secondary school that I realised that most girls have at least one pair of jeans. As soon as I came back from school after that first day I asked Mum to take me out and buy me a pair of jeans, I so much wanted and needed to fit in.

Since then I have surrounded myself with a group of five really good friends. We're all really close – there's nothing we don't know about each other. But within that group, my best friend, Amy, is special. At last, I found that special friend, the one I'd longed for better than my imaginary friends because she was real. She's very chatty and gets on with everyone – so much so, I sometimes think my mum likes her more than me!

Amy's family is from Hong Kong originally but they moved over here when she was eleven and I met her soon after she'd arrived. I had to save her from another crowd – some girls at school who were real trouble. She's been a real best friend to me ever since. She always seems to know the right time, place or thing to say or do something. Of course, she can be annoying too – she couldn't be a real best friend without the annoying parts of her. But she's also a great negotiator, and I always think of her as very stable.

Nothing ever got between us until, well, there was this boy . . . It's so predictable – it's always going to be about a boy.

We both met Joe at the same time at a party and though I didn't want a boyfriend I found myself really liking him – straight away, in that indefinable way that you can with a boy.

After that, we would all hang out together. I thought Joe and I were getting on really well. The problem was that Amy had felt the same way towards him and before I knew it, Amy was telling me that she really liked him too. It was terrible. I didn't know what to do. Amy hadn't been out with a boy before, she'd never even kissed one. I thought she was joking, but slowly I realised that she wasn't. They'd been online together and really liked each other. Then I noticed she started to change her fashion, started wearing shorter skirts whenever we saw him. It got a little weird.

Then, the worst thing happened. The day I was going to ask him out, he asked her out. She didn't want to accept because she knew I liked him but I convinced her to say yes. In the end, I thought they really were much better suited to each other than I would have been with him. Why? Because they are both seriously sarcastic – they are hilarious together.

At first I thought I couldn't be friends with them,

but you have to stand back and see the wider picture. Amy is more important to me than a boyfriend, because we've gone through so much together. There's nothing you could do to separate us, we'd never betray each other.

Joe has become part of our group and he and Amy are so sweet together. Amy is always expecting that he's going to cheat on her, but it's obvious to everyone else that he is so in love with her. I have to convince her that it's not going to happen, that it's all in her mind. Sometimes I feel like their relationship counsellor but they've been together for five months and it's going well. In a way Joe is like a mix of me and Amy.

All of us have applied for the same university, doing different courses. I've just found out that I've got in to do film studies and I'm so happy. It would be great if we could all continue being together, but if we don't, I think we'll still be friends.

Now that I'm seventeen I think that the thing I've learned about friendship is that the more time and effort you invest in it, the longer the friendship is going to last. Sometimes making that effort seems extremely difficult for me – writing letters, e-mails and stuff, for example, because I'm dyslexic, but also when boys come along. It's so easy to think they are going to be the thing that's going to make you happier than anything else, which is just rubbish.

In the end I'm sure it's worth it, all the effort and maturity! No, seriously, it's like anything you put effort into that you care about. It's the caring that makes things come out better in the end.

THE OLDEST AND BEST

KATE HOEY – LABOUR MP AND FORMER MINISTER FOR SPORT

I grew up in the middle of nowhere on a small organic farm in the countryside in the 1950s. We were very poor and I realise now what a struggle it must have been for my parents. My sister was a year and a half older than me, and terribly bright, always studying. We fought a lot, the way sisters do who are very different, but we were and are still very close. My father was always reading. He was a very clever man, he knew so much about the stars, other planets and Earth. He taught me to read the night sky, and I would sit outside with him in the evening and marvel at the brightness of Orion and know that it was Venus that was shining down on us. My father knew the name of every bird and tree, plant and animal and he was always teaching my sister and me things when we were growing up. He taught me about the importance of friendship with nature and your surroundings.

Most of the time, I was so busy doing farm duties, there wasn't much time outside of school for close friendships. I would walk the mile up the road to home, from where the bus dropped me after school, and Mum would always be there in the kitchen and I would rush to tell her all about my day – we were very close. There is such a definite routine on a farm, you know what you're meant to be doing every part of each day. Even in the school holidays, my days were filled with helping in whatever was going on at that time of the season on the farm. We were a very happy family.

In those days there was no Internet, and the telephone was for emergencies only, so friends had to live nearby. School and home were always a long way from each other. Junior school was just too far away. We were out in the middle of the countryside. And if your parents run a farm, they're much too busy working and occupied looking after the animals to be ferrying you about to friends' houses. So the animals become your best friends – the cats and dogs, as well as the farm animals.

I would talk to all the animals. There was a horse I would ride who was actually meant for the ploughing, and then there were the cows, and the chickens and pigs. Pigs are the most intelligent and sensitive of creatures, it felt like they really understood what you were thinking, feeling and talking about and I spent a lot of time with them.

It wasn't really until I got to secondary school that I became best friends with two girls called Hilary and

Margaret. Margaret was very pretty, fair, kind and with such a gentle, jolly nature. Everyone wanted to be friends with Margaret and she seemed to be aware of this, and almost actively shared herself amongst people. Boys were always asking her out too. She was terribly popular. She came from a very middle-class home – a very different sort of home from mine.

Hilary was darker, determined and less gregarious than Margaret. Her family were quite easily the richest in the area. When she was seventeen and as soon as she could drive, her parents bought her a car and we'd drive out to Saturday night dances in it. We'd have a whale of a time! Money and the difference of our family circumstances didn't seem to matter at all. I understood when I asked for things from my parents that they would often have to say no, as we didn't have the money. I was conscious of my friends' wealth, but I wasn't ever envious. I was just glad that Hilary had a car and was happy to drive us all around.

When I think back to how we were as teenagers we seemed so naïve, young and innocent compared to girls today. We remained children for much longer and I don't know if it was because we lived in the country or because it was so many years ago. For instance, though we had a phone, I wouldn't have dreamed of just sitting and chatting on the phone for hours to my friends, we couldn't afford it. The phone was used simply to impart information, not as a social instrument. So in the holidays I didn't really talk to Hilary or Margaret. But I was still very busy. We didn't have a television, I read a lot and then of course there were all the farm chores to be done.

Our school was a mixed grammar school, and though there was Hilary and Margaret and myself, there were groups and crowds of other friends that we would hang around with too. I was the only really sporty one of the three of us – I was always very keen on sports and athletics, and more boys tended to be involved with that. After school and at lunch we would go and train for track, but I didn't see those boys as anything other than friends, but my best friends were always Margaret and Hilary. Of course there are always girls who have just one best friend and they walk about like Siamese twins, but I have always enjoyed having multiple friendships.

I don't think as we became teenagers that Hilary and Margaret and I even realised that we were becoming women. We giggled a lot together but we didn't discuss sex and make-up, though of course we would go on dates and sit around during break the next day discussing the details.

"So – did you kiss him, or hold his hand?"

"What was he like?"

"And then what happened?"

And on Saturday night there was the dance and we would go to a big hall and stand on one side waiting to be asked to dance by the boys on the other side of the hall. It was all very thrilling.

Hilary started going out with a school prefect when we were seventeen. After school they got engaged and were about to be married when Hilary called it off, which was very outrageous in those days. Margaret got engaged and trained to be a teacher and went on to marry. I went to university, studied sport and became head of the student union. It was all very 'local girl made good'. We were each of us going in different directions and I suppose our friendships could have ended, but thankfully they didn't.

You don't realise at the time when you become friends that forty-odd years later you might still be sitting down and having lunch with these friends who have known you for what feels like your whole life. And the extraordinary thing is you feel nothing has changed. I still call them whenever I go back to see my mother in Northern Ireland and we get together.

Hilary worked her way through the health service and is a senior civil servant. Neither Hilary nor I have had children, but Margaret has. She settled down and had a family and then went back to work as a teacher. When I was sixteen, my mother had my baby brother and I was so involved with looking after him and playing with him I really think I got all the broodiness out of me, but Margaret's children I'm very close to. I still can't quite believe how old they are now, we are, and that all this time has disappeared from when the three of us first became friends and were at school together.

I do think supportive friendships are so important if you're going to succeed in life. Of course your family and schools matter too, but when you have these long friendships, there's nothing you have to explain, you've known each other so well for so long; it's easy.

Margaret and Hilary are still my best and oldest friends today.

ON THE NEXT MOUNTAIN

GISELLE, 15

The year before last, when I was thirteen, I got my first boyfriend, Neil. I thought he was lovely, as handsome and lovely as I could hope for or dream of. I thought I was lucky to have a boy like Neil. That he actually wanted to go out with me was almost unbelievable. I remember praying to God and saying, "Thank you so much for giving me Neil," because he was like a present. The best present I'd ever been given.

Neil was beautiful to look at, with really shiny black hair and eyes so blue that gazing into them was like looking up into a summer's sky. He was funny too – you know, he could make anyone laugh, and he was pretty smart as well, had the answers to everything. All that and he dressed really well and he was fourteen – a year older than me.

Julie has been my best friend since I was ten. When Julie and I met we just clicked – there was no one I liked spending time with as much as her. It was really funny because at around the same time my mum had just met the man who was soon to become my step-father, so she was always off with him. My dad had left when I was about five. I can't really remember him because one day he was there and then the next he just never came back. I suppose Julie was my first best friend. Anyway, I know her better than my mum practically.

But there was a problem. Julie thought Neil was awful. It was horrible. She kept running him down, saying he was a loser, stupid and cheap. It upset me to hear her talk about anyone I liked in that way, but especially since she knew just how much I liked him. Julie didn't have a boyfriend.

Julie and I had been such close friends and spent so much time together for so long, we were practically related. I'd start a sentence and she'd finish it. Of course we had our own private language that we used if there was anyone else around. We always shopped for clothes together – we'd get on the bus from our village, and go into the city together for the day and we would buy similar clothes, matching or complementing each other. We'd even plan how we'd wear our hair the night before going to school, so the next day we would both be wearing our hair in pigtails or plaits. The same coloured socks, shoes, school uniform. Our teachers would say, "I can't tell you two apart. Now which one of you is Julie and which is Giselle?" I swear Julie knew more about me than my mum did, we talked more than Mum and me; which is why I knew she knew how much I liked Neil.

I had been going steady with Neil for about four weeks when disaster struck. Julie and Neil were round mine, we'd been watching a DVD and we were going to go down the park since the sun seemed to be appearing after hours of rain. I went upstairs to get a jacket and when I came down the stairs there was this weird, I don't know, kerfuffle – an awkward, odd movement and silence going on between them in the hall. Something was going on but I didn't know what. I looked from one to the other and they both looked away and turned around embarrassed. It was peculiar; I'd only gone to get a jacket. We walked to the park together and then Neil went to play football with his mates. Julie and I stood on the sidelines and watched them.

"You're awful quiet, Julie. Nothing wrong is there?" I said to her. And then she just blurted it out: "Neil kissed me."

I was so surprised I didn't say anything. "He kept asking for a kiss, Gissy. I didn't know what else I was supposed to do. Gissy, I'm sorry, honest, I'm sorry, but he kept asking me to kiss him." I turned around and walked away and down the road, I didn't know what else to do.

I sat for a long time on the end of my bed looking

out the windows towards the mountains. Looking at the mountains helps me think. The mountains stand strong and still around our valley in Wales, whilst the stream runs down them, the grass grows over them and the sheep graze on top. In the winter, the snow covers and freezes them, and in the summer the sun scalds them and leaves their rocks baking warm. Mostly the wind blows past them and the rain pours on to them. It had started raining again, drizzling down the window. I didn't know what to think except, I suppose, I learned that we have to be a bit like mountains. Now that sounds stupid, but what I mean is, all sorts of things happen to us in life but we have to try and remain still, as still as mountains, to be the strong ones.

Julie came to call for me later but I told Mum I didn't want to see her and I locked my room. She stood outside and shouted through the door, "Gissy, it's not my fault. Honest, I didn't want to, but he kept asking." Why do people always say 'honest' when they're lying?

I just didn't know why they had to do it in my house. If I had not gone upstairs for a jacket would it ever have happened? Was it my fault for leaving them alone in the hall? My fault for being worried about being cold and needing a jacket? If I'd got a cardigan instead, would that have made things different? Or worn different jeans that day, or if it hadn't rained?

There are all these factors that make things different but if you keep thinking about the 'what if's', you can drive yourself bloomin' bonkers.

I didn't want to see Julie, or anyone. That is easier said than done where I live, because as soon as you step outside our door you're on the main street see, and Julie lives that close. So I stayed in my room and listened to music and that always makes things a bit better. Mum asked what was wrong with me, but I couldn't tell her; I knew she wouldn't understand. How could anyone understand unless they had been betrayed by the two people that meant the most to them? Being betrayed by one is bad enough, but not two of your favourite people, not together. I knew I had to speak to Julie some time, but what about Neil?

Julie must have said something to Neil, because in the end he came and apologised to me. Then he did this whole thing, apologised to both of us in front of everyone in the street. That was a bit embarrassing. I couldn't go out with him again after all that, you know? From that moment on, Julie and I said that we'd go out with boys who were mates. That way we wouldn't ever be put in the same position again.

When Julie started going out with William, and I started going out with John. It's been like that for about six months. It was alright until Julie just told me last week that she was pregnant by William. I wanted to be happy for her, but we're only fifteen. I wasn't really ever that keen on John, it was just that he was William's mate, so I'm finishing with him. I suppose I went out with him to keep Julie happy.

I'm not sure what's going to happen with Julie any more. I'd like to say we'd stay friends for life but now she's always bunking school, like this was the excuse she was looking for, know what I mean? I mean what we will have left in common? I want to go to university, I don't want children. Besides, Sue and I have started hanging out together. Sue can be a right laugh and I positively know whatever happens, she'd never kiss a boy just because he asked her. She's not like that. I'm not even sure it wasn't Julie who kissed Neil in the first place.

But as I said, lots of things happen to everyone, and what happened with Julie was really important at the time, but lots more things will happen to me and, just like the mountains, you have to be strong. You can't let things affect you, not deep down, not to change you. You never see a mountain crumbling and falling to pieces just because the sheep wanders off on to the next mountain, do you? Of course not, that would be just plain daft. It's not the mountain's fault that the sheep want to go and eat grass somewhere else, is it?

A Picture In My Head

Daisy de Villeneuve – illustrator
and graphic novelist
www.daisydevilleneuve.com

She was my best friend. She was sixteen when I met her and I was a bit older, but the age didn't make a difference because she had this incredible bubbly, energetic, fun personality. That's what I thought when I first met Lara at college. We'd both grown up in the same part of the same city but never met, and when we finally did we were inseparable. Nothing came between us. She had a boyfriend, Sam, whom she'd known since they were kids and who had been her boyfriend for two years. However, he'd gone off to uni by that point, because he was older than her too. I didn't have a boyfriend.

One weekend, Lara called me up when Sam wasn't around and asked me to go to a party. I really didn't want to – I was feeling a bit miserable and had just started my period – but she kept on cajoling me. She insisted that it would be really fun and that a boy that I quite fancied would be there, plus loads of her other friends were going too. I think sometimes she used me as an excuse to go out and get off with other boys behind Sam's back because she also mentioned that another boy she really liked was going too.

So, reluctantly, I went over to her house and when I turned up, two boys were already over there, the one I'd always liked, Tim, and a guy called Mike. It turned out that neither of them wanted to go to the party either. Tim asked if I'd go to the pub with them instead, and I at once said yes.

"But you can't! I mean, you said you were going to come to the party with me!" Lara was furious with me.

"But you said there were going to be loads of people you knew there and it was going to be great. I'm not feeling well and I'm just not in a mad party mood. Sorry," I said, and she seemed to accept that. Tim and I left for the pub, and Lara went to the party with Mike.

I was really pleased to be alone with Tim because I'd had a crush on him for quite a while, and when we got off together that night I was really happy. I thought he was totally gorgeous.

The next day Lara called me up to cross-examine me about Tim – she wanted all the details. But when I told her that Tim and I were now going out, she went ballistic. "I thought you were miserable and weren't feeling that well?"

"I was and I'm not, but why should that have stopped anything happening?"

"Well . . . well you should have said no, because . . . because, you knew that I always liked him!"

"What? You never said anything! Anyway, you already have a boyfriend – what about Sam?"

"That's my business."

I saw Tim a few more times, but we argued a lot. I didn't like his odd attitude towards me, so we stopped seeing each other. The situation wasn't helped by Lara, who rang me up constantly to tell me gossip about Tim, about how she was sure he already had a girl-friend, how she'd seen him out with other girls in town and about his past reputation.

Then a few weeks after we split up, she called me up and said she really urgently had to talk to me, could we meet up? So I met her at a café, and in her usual way, she turned up without any money, so I bought the drinks. I knew what she was going to say, I just knew it, and I even had to pay for the drinks so she could tell me!

"You'll never guess what, Daisy! You know I told you Tim had a new girlfriend? Well ... I think, I think it's me!" She squealed excitedly. "But how come you never told me he was such a lousy kisser?"

I was both upset and flabbergasted. She seemed totally oblivious to any feelings I might have had for Tim, and the way she was behaving as a friend. Instead she started going on to me about how much she wished she was me, that my life was so perfect. That if she could be me there was a chance that she could be happy. That her father had always preferred his second family to her, and wouldn't even let her meet them. That so many things had gone wrong in her life, so many bad things had happened to her, but at least she had a friend like me, one that understood her and her mess. I left the café feeling like I'd been robbed, but as if I'd been told I should feel happy about it, because what had been stolen had gone to someone who needed it more than me.

Lara continued seeing Tim, and also kept asking me round. I refused all her invitations; I wasn't a glutton for punishment.

I guess I felt sorry for her – she was a mess. She never seemed to know what she wanted. She was still seeing her old boyfriend, Sam, and said she loved him but couldn't be faithful to him. Eventually she and Tim split up. After that, we kept on bumping into each other and I kept a friendly face, but we never discussed the T-word. That way we could make believe our friendship was still there. Two years later, nothing had changed in our circumstances that much, and we were walking in the market and talking and she asked me in the way girls do . . .

"Who's the best person you've ever kissed?"

I couldn't answer because I don't really think like that. I mean, it's a relationship, not just kissing, that makes things good between two people. I asked her, "What about you?" and she said, "Oh, that's easy, it was always Tim."

I felt she had broken our unspoken agreement. I couldn't help myself I had to say, "Oh. I thought he was the worst."

"Well, he's not. Actually he always told me that he never even really wanted to be with you."

And in that moment, I saw a picture of them so clearly in my head, of them lying together talking about me, dissecting me. I felt so utterly betrayed. I couldn't believe she didn't understand that I might just be a little bit hurt by what she had done, and that I might feel thoroughly betrayed by her. She was supposed to be my friend but if you can't even empathise with a friend, what sort of friendship is it?

The odd thing is that still today, after all those years have gone by – all ten of them – she *still* sees me as one of her closest friends. It's difficult because we both moved to London and still mix among the same crowd socially, and also for work. She still tells me secrets about what she gets up to. How she loves the excitement of being unfaithful and yet is too insecure to leave her boyfriend – poor Sam, who's actually become really successful in New York. Oh, and how she really loves him flying her over for visits. God knows why he stays with her. They're more like brother and sister than boyfriend and girlfriend. I feel that I'm holding all her secrets. She tells me that I'm the only one who doesn't judge her – I don't, but it's because I don't care. I mean, I can't because I'm never going to trust her ever again. It's not as if I'm going to tell her any of my secrets, is it? I wondered at first if Lara behaved as she did because she was so young at the time, but now I just think she might have something really, really wrong with her.

FOREIGNERS

DAISY, 16

I was twelve, and I'd just arrived in France and was starting a new school. I was so nervous – I couldn't speak French and didn't know anyone, not a soul. It wasn't just starting a new school, we'd just moved to a new country too and everything was so different. We used to live in Ireland and, believe me, Ireland is not like France.

When the teacher introduced me to the class, she said, "We have another new girl who also doesn't speak French." I was relieved, except this girl didn't speak English either – she was Russian. The minute we saw each other we clicked and from the beginning of that first day we became best friends. We saw each other every day while we learned how to speak French together. I also taught her how to speak English – somehow, even without language, we managed to communicate and make each other laugh.

Within a couple of months we were so close we even rang each other first thing in the morning before we met at the bus stop to go to school, then we sat next to each other through classes and played together after school. We became known as 'Daisy-and-Diana' at school, as there was never one of us without the other.

But at the end of our first term, we got our exam results and suddenly Diana's mother said she wasn't allowed to see me outside of school any more, not until her grades got better. Her mother insisted that she had to have one hundred per cent in every subject, and her punishment for not having achieved that in her first term was not to see her friends, which meant me.

We saw as much of each other as we could during school hours. Even though we weren't allowed to hang out together after school, we really did our best to keep our friendship together.

Diana is really naturally pretty with brown hair and quite a serious face, but she does dress rather oddly. She always wears skirts, never trousers, and these skirts have got shorter and smaller, her tops tinier and her heels higher the older we've got. Very different to my style. But what do clothes matter when you've got so much else in common with a friend? However, when she dyed her hair blond and started wearing tiny thongs with her mini-skirts, I had to say something. The whole school was talking about her and neither the boys or girls liked her any more. I mean, we were thirteen years old and she was walking about looking like a hooker! But however much I tried to suggest that maybe jeans might be a good idea, or a longer skirt or dress, she stuck to her reality of tiny skirts and small tight tops.

What was also odd was that though her mother was really strict with her grades she was very liberal about everything else. Her mother didn't mind her dying her hair or wearing these tarty clothes, or staying out really late at night – as long as she achieved one hundred per cent grades, anything was all right by her. Diana really didn't understand how unpopular she was making herself by dressing in this provocative way, and I didn't like the way everyone made fun of her, because underneath all that she was a really nice girl. Perhaps she was desperate for attention, but she didn't realise that the attention she got from wearing these clothes was the wrong kind.

When this seventeen-year-old dumb boy (who was held back two years) said he fancied her and asked her out, she thought it was really cool because he was five years older than us. But he wasn't going out with her for her personality or even because she was pretty, but as a bet – he was making fun of her. When I told her what was happening, she'd just reply, "No, you don't understand, Daisy. He really likes me." She just wouldn't listen. Of course the whole thing ended really badly, with him dumping her in front of everyone in assembly. I felt for her but she still didn't get it; didn't understand what her reputation had become.

I was always more popular at school than Diana, but I suppose I stuck by her because our personalities were so similar in many ways. We talked for hours and we laughed even more. By that time, Diana's mother allowed us to see each other out of school again – so long as her grades didn't slip. We used to get up at five a.m. every morning and go down to the beach and practise surfing so that when summer arrived we wouldn't be terrible at it. We both have loads of energy and determination. We thought nothing could keep us from being friends. So when she told me one day that her family was moving to another village, I said it didn't matter, we'd still be friends at school. Then one day she changed schools to be nearer to her new home, and we saw each other less and less often.

One weekend she came to stay and then declared that she was going to see her ex-boyfriend, because he'd asked her over.

"Are you mad?" I said. 'After all that happened?'

"He says he still likes me and I want to see him."

"And you're listening to him over me! I've been your friend for three years and you've known him, what, off and on, a couple of months? And what about the way he treated you, and the way he finished with you?"

"I knew you'd be like that. You don't know what love's like," she told me angrily before she left to go to his place. All I knew was that she'd chosen to spend her time with this jerk who'd humiliated her in front of everyone, rather than with me.

Things went downhill from there with our friendship. We hardly saw each other, and when I called her at home, her mum always made up some excuse for why I couldn't speak to Diana – she was in the shower, or busy feeding the hens, or out with her new friends from her new school – and then when we did speak our conversations became so dull it was as though we'd never shared anything, never had that connection; it was really weird. She'd say something like, "Hey, guess what? I got a hundred per cent in my maths." And I'd be thinking, "What's new? You always get a hundred." But I'd say, "Wow! Really? Well done." We were just having these fake conversations.

The very last time we had a proper conversation I asked her straight: "Why can't you see me? Why don't you ever have the time for me any more?"

And she replied, "I can't. It's better this way. I have to have my other friends." And finally she said, "I just don't want to stay friends with you any more."

And now when we pass each other in town, it's like we occupy completely different worlds. We might say a cursory "Hi", but basically it's like we've never known each other.

She's sixteen and still parading around with her itsy-bitsy skirts, trying to get attention by pouting, and she still doesn't understand that it's negative attention, really negative. I understand now what my Mum meant when she told me to be careful of Diana and that she could get me mixed up in bad stuff in town. Mum did like her at the beginning but she's changed so much. I don't feel that I've changed, I mean, I feel basically the same, but I must have I suppose, because I used to really like her, and we had so much in common. Now, I don't think we could ever be friends. The last time I saw Diana, she really reminded me of someone, and then I realised who. She's just like Paris Hilton, but not in a good way.

BACK TO LIFE

KATY, 18

My granny brought me up. Of course my mum had
me and looked after me, but it was Gran who always
picked me up from nursery and then school, because
Mum was always working. On ill days and holidays
she looked after me all day, every day, not just after
school and before Mum came back from work.
Sometimes we went to playgrounds, or gardens, to her
flat or to ours.

I know she was old, but nothing made me think of
her as a granny. She was always full of smiles and
laughing, games and mischief. I had to think sometimes about which one of us was the child, she could
be *so* childish. She loved talking about rude things;
making farting noises on a bus was about as funny as
you could get with her.

Yes, she had wrinkles, crêpe-like skin crossed with a
million lines covered her nose, hands and chin. She
said her extra fat was my fault, that she had grown it
especially for me so that she would have a comfy
granny lap, so that I could 'snug' into her when I was

small. She often used words that seemed to be just ours, because I never heard them anywhere else. We would 'totty down' in the sand, make and eat 'blanket' pies. All of which sound so weird without her saying them . . .

Gran might have been chubby but it never stopped her from chasing after me on my bicycle, or playing hopscotch, jumping in puddles on 'wind-walloping' afternoons, or running in and out of the waves on 'sun-washing' days at the seaside. She liked the sound of words, she liked adventures. If she found a word she really liked she'd say it over and over until it meant nothing, but it made us laugh.

It wasn't just silly words and jokes with Gran, I can't tell you the amount of things she taught me – how to make this or how to draw that, reading and writing, why the sky was blue and what the world was about. She had all the time in the world for me and my endless questions, and I'm sure I was irritating.

Honestly, every day I would run out from school to meet her and she would always be there, a smile as wide as a slice of watermelon, arms outstretched to bundle me up and lift me to her lips to kiss. "Hello, sausage. How's my little chickchick been today?" she'd say, and laugh this low deep chuckle. I would laugh back and say, "Peep peep." I'd hug her, my nose to the side of her neck where I could sniff her warm lavender perfume.

As I got older I'd reprimand her, say, "Oh silly Granny. I am not a sausage! I'm an eight-year-old girl."

Eventually I told her to stay at home because I was too old to have her collect me from school. I know she was disappointed – I saw her smile slide away – but I always went to see her after school.

As she got older she might not have been able to help me with my maths homework, but she always knew how to make me laugh.

When I started secondary school I began to make friends with a group of girls, Rosie, Louise and Henri, but none of them seemed to understand why I wanted to spend so much time with Gran. Their grandparents were all either dead or living in another place and they'd see them once a year, if that. Henri's grandparents lived in Spain and Rosie's gran lived in Jamaica. They'd tease me, so eventually I told them Gran was ill and I had to go and look after her. Still they tried to make me go hang out with them instead of spending all my time with her.

"How are your friends, Katy? You don't have to always come here after school," she'd say to me. "Unless you want to, of course."

The thing about Gran was she understood me better the older I got, better than I understood myself. She would always be sympathetic to my feelings, never pushing too much to find out what was wrong if I'd had an argument with Rosie, Louise or Henri, or

Mum. I was always having huge fights with Mum about stupid things like tidying my bedroom or washing up. Gran would wait for me to open up and afterwards she'd never tell me what to do unless I asked her. We had a different link from the friends I had at school. It wasn't just all the years we had spent together, it wasn't like Mum and me – Gran was more of an extension of me, she understood how I felt and what I needed more than anyone else. When Mum and I went on holiday alone one year, I missed her so much that I cried for two whole weeks. From then on Gran always came with us.

As she got older, Gran's hips got bad. She always blamed it on the rationing during the Second World War, when there hadn't been enough milk. I'd always drop in on my way home from school to see if she needed anything. The lifts were always breaking down and even two flights of stairs from the basement entrance could be hard for her.

It was almost four years ago now, the day when I rang on the doorbell and shouted through the silly letterbox with the bright yellow smiley face she'd let me paint on it when I was nine. I could hear the radio, but when there was no answer I used the key she'd given me: "My home is your home," that's what she always said. I thought she was probably out in the garden – she loved her garden, the apple tree in autumn, the strawberry plants running over the whole of one bed, and lots of sunflowers and marigolds. She loved yellow. I walked in and called out, "Gran? Yoo-hoo. It's me, Katy." The garden door was open, the pink curtain billowing out from the breeze, a bird singing in the tree and the radio announcer saying it was five o'clock and time for the news. It's funny the things you remember so, so precisely. I looked around the room and then I saw her by my feet; she'd fallen, collapsed, and I knew she was dead. I just knew it. I tottied down by her and held her hand in my hands, pressed it to my cheek. It was cold, cold as stone; no pulse. I got up to fetch a blanket, one of the patch-work ones we'd made together a few Christmases before, and a pillow to put under her head, and I sat there talking to her for ages, telling her how much I loved her, how it was going to be OK. Then I got up and called Mum and the ambulance. It seems mad now.

I couldn't go to school after that. I couldn't do any-thing.

"Gran wouldn't have wanted you not to go to school what with exams, or to be so miserable," Mum said, but I replied, "How can you go on like nothing's happened?" Mum said, "That's unfair. I don't, Katy, I just go on. That's all."

I felt more alone than anyone should be allowed to feel at fourteen. I felt I'd been deserted and that there was no one in the world who would ever understand me, or love me again as Gran had, and I didn't know why nobody seemed able to understand that. And then the rows really started with Mum. I remember her screaming at me, "You can't feel worse than me. She was *my* mum, not yours," and both of us crying, neither of us listening to each other, just shouting, lots of shouting.

After the funeral we just ignored each other, days went by and weeks, then school started to ring up and Mum started going ballistic again.

"Do you want me to be locked away in prison because of your truanting? Is that what you want?" she demanded. Of course, I didn't, but really I couldn't care about anything, there wasn't the space.

Then one day Henri came round and rang on the door. I didn't want to see her, but Mum let her in and she came and knocked on my door and I let her in. We sat there not talking for ages, and then she said that everybody at school was really missing me, that it wasn't the same without me, and I told her how I couldn't feel or care about anything, or anyone. She listened and left. And then everyday for a week, she came after school, each day for a bit longer than the day before. Slowly she told me about her gran, and how she was always telling her off, for the clothes she wore and how she talked. And then I started to tell her about Gran. How much I loved her and how much I missed her, and all the things we did together and why she was so unique, like the best part of me. Henri admitted how jealous she was of that. I'll always remember she said I should be happy that I'd had anybody in life who loved me so much; who wasn't even my mum.

I knew she was right, and I knew my mum did love me. After that, I tried harder, and things started to come back together – I made up with Mum and started going to school again. Now I suppose Henri has taken over from my gran, she's definitely my best friend. It's horrible to think it took Gran dying to bring us together, but I like to think that it was more a present from Gran. I'll never forget the way that Henri brought me back to life, to living. She could have ignored me like the others, but she took the time and the effort to understand. She's a bit like Gran in a way, she's rude and we laugh a lot, but unlike Gran we can go out clubbing together. What else do you need from a best friend? I think Gran would definitely approve.

IRISH IDYLL

JASMINE GUINNESS – MODEL AND CO-FOUNDER
OF THE CHARITY, CLOTHESLINE
www.clothesline.org

Zita and I have known each other since birth, my birth quite literally. Her very first memory, when she was two, is of seeing me as a new baby; and mine is of seeing her surrounded by pots of chocolate mousse that she was eating at my fourth birthday party, looking very happy indeed.

We grew up together, both living on my grandparents' farm outside of Dublin in the south of Ireland. Her parents were best friends with my grandparents and lived at the gatehouse – my grandparents lived in the main house, whilst I lived with my parents in the garden cottage. My parents were pretty young – seventeen and twenty-one – when they had me, their first child, and much of the time our house was like a teenage party, whilst Zita's parents were quite a bit older and they had another, older daughter, Poppy. I spent so much time at Zita's house that I even had my own bed there. I really adopted their family as mine; Zita and Poppy were my big sisters.

We had such enormous freedom on the farm, no

constraints. It was our own playground and we were all tomboys, climbing trees and making dens, galloping around fields racing our very fat, pretend ponies, until one day we were old enough to ride on our own ponies and we didn't have to pretend; we were doing it for real racing each other around the farm.

Zita was always amazingly creative and always busy with some plan or other. She was also very clever and very bossy and I was her willing accomplice. Of course we got into fights, like sisters – we'd argue and go off to sulk separately. Our arguments lasted only as long as we could stand being without each other. We were practically inseparable.

Zita and I went to the same nursery school and then junior school, but because she was two years older than me, she left and went off to secondary before me and I was left alone at junior for another two years. I felt like I'd been deserted. Suddenly Zita seemed terribly sophisticated with all her new friends – going off on the bus together and into the city on her own, and I felt both young and intimidated by all of them. Yet as soon as the holidays arrived, Zita and I were back where we always were, hanging out, lying in fields. Her dad would let us listen to his fantastic and huge collection of records from reggae to punk, rockabilly to ska – we'd jump around dancing for hours. But her parents were great at doing normal family kids' stuff with us in a way that my parents didn't, like taking us to the cinema or on outings.

It wasn't always easy, there were perils in having an older friend. Sometimes she would suggest great ideas to me like, "Jasmine, why don't we draw all over each other's faces for fun. You first." And I sat there and she drew all over my face in biro and when I asked if it might be my turn to do it to her, she ran away laughing, and I burst into a rage of tears. But really our only bone of contention was a shared competitive spirit – mostly about racing our ponies and whose could go faster.

At eleven I went to boarding school, but always came home at the weekends and went straight to Zita's house. It drove my poor parents mad. Mum would have made a special effort to cook lunch or dinner and I wouldn't come home till dark. But my parents were extremely understanding of me wanting to be with Zita and Poppy, brilliant even. They let me make my own decisions on where I wanted to be and never made me do anything I didn't want to do. The only thing they were strict on was to always say 'please' and 'thank you' and to eat all my dinner on the odd occasion I was there. Having kids of my own now, I understand how upsetting it must have been for them, never really having me around because I more or less lived with Zita's family.

When Zita became a teenager, our friendship was

sometimes a little difficult. She had her first teenage party at fourteen. I found it terrifying, with lots of cider and boys, and suddenly I felt very young. Boys always fancied Zita because she was so very motivated, vivid, interested and interesting, and she had a blanket of beautiful long blond-brown hair. She was growing up and I was still just a child.

When it came to boys and us, we only ever fancied the same one once – when I was ten, and Zita must have been twelve. When he seemed to like her better than me, I was terribly jealous of her – extremely jealous – for the first and only time. But we soon realised that this boy was toying with us both, playing us off against the other, so we said, "To hell with him!" And it just made us better friends.

In our later teens we grew back together again. We'd dress up together, and streak our hair. We always had fun, whatever we were doing – making things, or just talking – so that I was truly devastated when during her year off after secondary school, aged seventeen, she went to work for a year in America as an au pair. Suddenly, I had no one to follow around, and I had to learn to rely on myself and carve out my own friendships without Zita doing it for me.

It was hard, but since then we've been through a lot of patches where we'll go our separate ways, and then join back together again. Like the time we were both at college and we were both living with our first boyfriends, and then we finished with them both in the same week and moved into my grandparents' London flat together that was a fantastic time of parties and going out but always having Zita to share it all with. After college I went off to model in New York, then we were apart for three years, because Zita remained in London. When I became pregnant I decided to fly back to Ireland to have the baby. Zita had already moved back there, working, so we had returned to the place of our childhood again. At that point we founded the charity called Clothesline which organises fashion shows and dress sales with the money going to help community-based projects for people with AIDS in sub-Saharan Africa.

If the charity didn't already demand us to be constantly in touch by phone and e-mail, everything else keeps us connected. Zita lives only three streets from me now, her cousin is my fiancé, and she's godmother to my first son, Elwood. We've always said one day we'll return to Ireland, so we can be grumpy old women, growing old, living together again on my grandparents' farm with her parents and my grandparents, that's the dream; the idyll.

The bond between Zita and me has never changed. We might have occupied ourselves with other friendships during term time when we were still at school, or when we were off in the world, but we still speak to each other every day, know what each other is thinking, and we've always finished each other's sentences. I just have to look at Zita's face and I know what's going on in her mind. Sometimes we spend all day together and she'll walk me back home and then as soon as she's back at her house, we'll be calling each other. I wonder how much we've spent on phone bills to each other over all these years?

I really believe that circumstance decided we'd be friends, but that we have also chosen to be friends, and it's the strength of our friendship, pride in each other, love and trust that has kept us together for all this time. And you know, I'm sure we'll grow old together.

Sophie Parkin has a degree in Fine Art, otherwise known as painting, chatting, writing, partying, chatting and having fun, and the occasional chat. In between chatting, she has had two children (Paris and Carson, who are great chatterers), has had painting exhibitions, run nightclubs, written grown-up novels and for newspapers, been a kids' Agony Aunt for AOL and cooked quite a lot.

She is also the author of two novels for teenagers: *French for Kissing*, and its sequel, *Mad, Rich and Famous*.